DENIED

The Search for Saudi Justice

By

James L. Dickson Jr.

This book is a work of non-fiction. Names and places have been changed to protect the privacy of all individuals. The events and situations are true.

ISBN: 1-4107-2448-4 (e-book)
ISBN: 1-4107-2449-2 (Paperback)
ISBN: 1-4107-5071-X (Dust Jacket)

This book is printed on acid free paper.

1stBooks - rev. 4/15/03

DEDICATION

This book is dedicated to the memory of Irma Gual Rexach.

PROLOGUE

The year is 1989 and I have just been invited to the Kingdom of Saudi Arabia, a land of mystery with closed borders and harsh strict Islamic rule. A desert land ruled by one man and his sons since 1932. I have been warned not to go but my interest in the country, the people and the opportunity presented to me made the decision an easy one. It would be nice to go to an environment with the lowest crime rate in the world, meet new people, take care of business and start a new project.

My initial excitement of going to Saudi Arabia soon gave way to the practical matter of such a trip. I needed to research material on this nomadic land. The available material fell into two categories: State Department material obtained from my senator and congressman's offices and the brochures from Saudi Arabia sent to me from Jeddah, Saudi Arabia. The congressional material did more to deter me than inform me, but the Saudi brochures were very informational and the more I read the better I felt. Yes, there could be problems. But there are problems with every new venture and once I am there, business is business, and I am well prepared to do more than expected.

The biggest obstacle was to get there quickly and with the proper credentials. I would enter the Kingdom of Saudi Arabia quietly, be able to keep my passport with me at all times so I could control my departure, and would pass through their security without any problems. From past travel experience I was confident that I had everything under control and anticipated few if any problems.

To enter Saudi Arabia is not easy because there are no tourist visas. Permission to enter is by one of two types of visas: you may receive a visa if you have an employment contract or if you are on a temporary business visit. To obtain a temporary business visa you must have a Saudi company sponsor you. This was done for me by my Saudi partner and is the best and safest visa to have because you do not have to surrender it, but must keep it with you at all times for proof of your legal right to be in the country. Those who have employment visas are given a resident permit and must surrender their passports and are not permitted to leave Saudi Arabia until they are issued an exit visa. Exit visas are sometimes very difficult to obtain and are issued only when the Saudi sponsor decides he wants you to leave.

After your visa is approved you must travel to one of four locations to physically obtain it and for me the best location was New York City. Arriving there I took a cab to the consulate office and was asked to come back later. No reason was given and I didn't ask for an explanation. I certainly didn't want to make an issue over such a trivial matter, especially after my Senator, Congressman and State Department literature warned me about the dangers involved in traveling to this restrictive country, and about security conditions that could well affect me as an American citizen. Returning later, the visa was obtained and my airplane tickets and itinerary would be sent to me as soon as a seat was available.

I packed my bags very carefully making sure I had no forbidden items, again reminded of the warnings from Senator D'Amato's office that traveling to Saudi Arabia was dangerous and the State Department wouldn't be able to help me. I was concerned but not worried for I had Clive and Irma Mohammed to guide me. Plus I was taking with me several big surprises for my partner. I had planned well and secured exclusive contracts for our business to represent American products not only in Saudi Arabia but also in other countries in the region. I was excited and filled with confidence that this business venture was off to a great start.

Arriving at the New York City airport and going immediately to the boarding area I was surprised to see all the passengers dressed in western clothes, socializing with each other in informal and happy tones. About one hour before boarding everyone except several Saudi Air Force officers went to the rest rooms and changed into the Saudi dress: the white "thobe" for the men and the black "abaaya" for the women. When they exited dressed properly for their trip back home a transfiguration had occurred and their mood and attitude was much different. The women were silent, avoiding eye contact, and the men were talking in a more somber manner.

The flight was uneventful except for a five star dinner with appetizers such as shrimp and lobster, several delicious entrees to choose from and a desert I can no longer remember. Drinks were bottled water for me from the moment I entered the plane until I arrived back in the good old' USA. Soon after dinner most of the

vi

passengers turned off their seat lights and with pillows and blankets settled in to sleep away the long journey. Sleep didn't come easy for me. My thoughts were filled with so many questions about the land, the people and the customs in this Arab country that not only didn't permit visitors but also didn't welcome outsiders. Would I be safe? Would my partner like me? Was it really a good idea to go all alone into an environment so much different than most of the world? An environment where being an American was a handicap and in some cases downright dangerous. I finally fell asleep without any answers and woke up to the hustle of activity around me. I was filled with excitement and was anxious to land and begin the work I had traveled so far to do.

About noon, twelve hours after take off, we landed in Jeddah, Saudi Arabia. The first thing I noticed were all the cars surrounding the plane. I was told that some passengers were being picked up by their drivers and their luggage was being transferred directly from the plane to their cars. The rest of us went quietly in line, following each other to the baggage pick up area. Finding my bags was easier than I anticipated and I was directed to the room with the customs inspectors. This is not the normal type of customs inspectors nor is it the typical inspection of luggage. Because the list of forbidden items is long and the penalties are sometimes severe, this is a very stressful time. Every item in your possession is suspect and any item not able to pass visual inspection is treated as a violation. Magazines are looked at page by page and offending pictures and passages are inked out. All books are inspected carefully. This is the house of Saud, the birthplace of Islamic religion. This is the country where Muhammad was born and where the holy cities of Mecca and Medina are located. All temptations must be left out of this holy land and the customs inspectors are to defend the borders and keep the sins of the world from entering.

I didn't pass inspection because I had a three to four minute video from a Maryland corporation explaining and visually showing their product line. The problem was simple. How did my customs agent know what was in the video tape?

The video was confiscated and I was taken out of the line and into a restraining area where the decision would be made on what to do with me until they had the time to look at the video. I was told I would probably be "held" for several days until they viewed the video and if it was as I explained I would be released to go about my business, and no, I could not make a phone call. Just sit in the restraining area until someone came for me. I was all alone and with no resources to appeal their decision. Then a small miracle happened. Dr. Clive Mohammed and my partner went looking for me and with their connections had been directed to where I was being detained. Clive spotted me and yelled for me to come to the door that was locked from the inside. After the excitement died down I was allowed to speak to Clive. My partner did his magic act and I was released into his custody. Wow! What a way to be introduced into a country you had been warned not to go to if you valued your freedom.

After the introductions I was taken to my hotel and in my room the three of us had a long meeting and plans for my visit were outlined day by day. Both Clive and my new partner were excited over all the products that were exclusively ours to be marketed in Saudi Arabia and the Gulf region. When Clive left to keep an appointment my partner stayed and phoned the hotel manager and asked him to come up to my room. When he arrived I listened to the instructions on how I was to be treated and was taken by complete surprise when the manager informed me he had ten thousand American dollars in his safe that were mine to spend while I was a guest here in Jeddah, and added that this was a bottomless amount. He further explained that whenever I spent any money that exact amount was immediately replaced and there was no limit on the amount I could spend. Talk about being well treated! I was beyond impressed with this generosity and before I could express my thanks the subject was changed and I was given a tour of the hotel. After this my partner left but not before telling the manager that he was leaving me under his personal care and as such I should be well treated. The event at the airport was behind me and I felt good about being here.

My days were filled with business and in the evenings I was invited to eat at various Saudi homes. I was treated better here, in Saudi Arabia, than it was ever possible to predict. In both business meetings and social meetings I was continually told that I was not an American and that I had to have some Arab heritage. This was meant as a compliment and I took it as such even though I protested each time and stated I was a proud American and most Americans I knew were very much like me.

There are four events that stand out about my visit that will give the reader some insight into the Saudi Arabia I was introduced to.

The first event was a social call during the day to a new dental office owned by three Saudi brothers. The floors were marble and there were separate areas for men and women. The brother in charge gave me a tour and asked me if I would be interested in going with him to Europe, where it would be my job to purchase equipment and furniture for these new offices.

My expenses would be paid by him for the ten days we would be gone and I would be paid ten percent of the costs of goods. Although I declined, Clive wrote to me when I was back in the States, repeating the offer to purchase this equipment, supplies and software package.

The second event was a social evening at a Sheikh's house, where dinner lasted over four hours. Numerous guests came from Jeddah and from Riyadh, but I was asked to sit at the place of honor, at the host's right side at the table. During the long meal the Sheikh and I had a long, private conversation about politics and about life in America. One very unusual detail was that both women and men sat at the same table, and the Sheikh's wife was very active in our conversation. She asked about business, social and educational issues in America. But her toughest question brought the whole room to silence. The question was: "What did I think about women not being permitted to drive in Saudi Arabia?" My question was: Should I support the law or talk about women's rights? No matter which approach or how soft I answered the question I was in trouble. How to answer and not offend was the real question. My answer certainly pleased my host as he leaned over to me and said: "That was the perfect answer." My reply had been very simple. "In America the people work hard and those who are very successful economically are rewarded with the luxury of employing drivers so their wives and children don't have the problems of driving, parking, and all the stress that goes with owning a car. Having a chauffeur is considered a huge perk that only a very few Americans can enjoy. In some families the women, if given the choice, will chose to have a chauffeur over expensive jewelry, furs and other luxuries they hold in high esteem. This is called 'having it made'." This answer closed this line of conversation and as I reflect back on my visit to Saudi Arabia this evening was the social highlight of my stay there.

The third event that stands out in my mind was a trip to the desert to visit a hospital. For this business call a Saudi hospital consultant accompanied me and my driver so I would be permitted to enter this restricted area. After getting lost for a short time we arrived at a parking lot that was well guarded with military personnel carrying automatic weapons. Arriving at the guard gate I was asked for my passport and tried to hand it to the guard. He completely ignored me as if I didn't exist and spoke in Arabic to my two companions. My Saudi consultant took the passport from my hand and showed it to the guard. This seemed to satisfy him, but when there was no visitor pass for me I was reluctant to continue. Assured that I was safe we entered the hospital and went through the same routine as we did on all my other business calls: a letter of introduction to the Saudi official in charge, a meeting with him and his assistant, coffee or tea served, meeting with other officials one at a time, until finally I met with the British person in charge of running the hospital.

It should be noted here that every hospital I went to, and there were many, either an American or a British firm were contracted to run the hospital. In this particular instance we had a meeting with this nervous Englishman who was accompanied by two or three Saudi officials standing nearby. The meeting was productive and we left in high spirits at the prospect that this hospital would soon become a customer. On the ride back to Jeddah I complimented Sami, my partner's son and our driver-guide today, on how every hospital we entered was so immaculately clean and how they had the latest equipment, with MRI machines, pneumatic tube systems, nursing station computers, automated mag stripe plastic card systems, information retrieving systems, up to date X ray department equipment, and on and on. To sum it all: the most modern and cleanest hospitals I had ever seen.

The fourth significant event in this trip was a visit to the United States Embassy in Jeddah. Entering through the front door was not allowed, according to the U.S. Marine stationed on guard there. So, with Sami guiding the way, we walked around the side of the building until we came to a temporary entrance. There I requested to enter and was refused. I presented my passport, a letter from my Senator and another letter from my Congressman, copies of which had been sent to the Embassy in advance of my trip. I was again refused entry with the comment: "Can't you see all the sandbags and problems we have here. Unless you can fully explain why it is necessary for you to come into the Embassy, you cannot enter." I tried to tell them that I would speak in private inside the Embassy and not in front of my Saudi companion. I was then threatened that they would call the guards if I didn't leave right away. Irritated, I walked away commenting that I thought all United States Embassies were for all American citizens. Because this was my first personal experience with an Embassy I thought maybe I didn't understand the functions and purposes, and that maybe in Saudi Arabia the rules were different. So I went back to work and decided I would soon leave this beautiful country where I was treated so special by the Saudis I met but not welcome in my American Embassy, which my tax dollars supported. The Embassy I had trusted to be helpful to me and a safe haven in case of trouble, was not available to this American citizen.

I increased the number of calls I was to make each day so I could leave before the start of the Hajj pilgrimage to Mecca. All government offices are closed during this ten day period and most business activities are curtailed. There are over two million Moslems from all over the world who arrive at the Jeddah airport and if you haven't planned well in advance it will be increasingly more difficult to get an airline ticket. With the help of my friends I finally secured a seat on what I was told was the last plane to New York City.

I finished my prearranged calls with plenty of time to sight see during the day and socialize during the evenings, and of course, take time out to go shopping for gifts for my family. My first stop was at Old Jeddah, which was only a short distance away from my hotel. The difference between the old city and the new one was like going back in time. Guided by Clive and Irma Mohammed I was able to make my purchases in one morning and then the three of us went to lunch at a very modern restaurant. My comments about the old and the new city and the interest I showed in wanting to know about how long it had taken to make all the changes guided the conversation for the rest of the afternoon into a history lesson for me. I asked questions about everything. There were no restrictions or topics that I could not and did not discuss. Clive told me about the political and business history while Irma told me about the restrictions for Saudi women in their private lives as well as in their public and social roles. This insight was much more than informative, it was downright fascinating. That evening I spent with my partner and his family. More history lessons, but this time from the perspective of the people who lived it from a vast desert up to 1990.

The history I learned was told by both the Saudis and by the Americans living there for an extended period of time. It is the story of one man and four of his forty-three sons. This man, the first king, Abdul Aziz ibn Saud successfully struggled and fought to unite all that is now Saudi Arabia into one country. He turned it from an arid desert with goat tents and a few cities with mud houses into a modern country with immense wealth; from camels to Rolls Royces; from mud houses to marble and stucco houses and palaces. Today, Saudi Arabia has a first class education system, outstanding health care with the latest equipment, plus an economic system that produces more wealth on a daily basis than is needed to run the Kingdom. Still there are problems. In this case the problems are too much oil. The more oil they produce, the more oil they discover.

Saudi oil has changed the politics of the world, especially in America. The history of the discovery of oil in Saudi Arabia and the way it has been used to influence political policy should be told by an expert. That one product could have so much influence might be difficult for most of us to believe, but entire economies throughout the world have risen and fallen on the price and availability of oil. Although this book is not about oil, a few facts will help the reader to understand that the project I was asked to undertake, Public Relations in the United States for Saudi Arabia, required that I have at least a knowledge of significant data as it pertained to the world view in general and the American view in particular of who and what is Saudi Arabia. A few events should make it clear how our American economy was affected by the politics and need for imported oil.

In the early 1930's, prior to World War II, an American engineer traveled to Saudi Arabia to gain permission to search for oil. Although the King had little faith in oil being discovered, he thought it would be a good idea to allow both the American's and British to believe there was oil. If he could get both searching for oil, he would be in a better position to gain economic aid from both countries. Although the Brit's thought it a long shot to find enough oil for the search to be profitable they also wanted to keep the American's out of Saudi Arabia, so they played the King's game.

King Abdul, a horse trader of great skill, played the British and the Americans against each other and offered the oil found to the highest bidder. America won and this made King Abdul happy because the British were colonialists wherever they went and always interfered with the government, while Americans only wanted the black gold, and this all Arabs could understand. Plus, it was easy to make a deal when you were quite sure there was no oil, especially if you could be paid in advance of finding it. The deal was made and the money paid in 1933. This was important because the global economies of the thirties had reduced the number of pilgrims traveling to Mecca and this pilgrimage was the primary source of the Kingdom's income, and money was scarce. Also, the King needed funds to keep his Kingdom together. Six years later the first oil was shipped to the States and this started a change that has rocked the world ever since.

During World War II America was supporting the allies with money and products and oil was very much in demand. We were depleting our own oil supply and needed exported oil. Saudi oil was the answer, so President Franklin D. Roosevelt changed his position on lend-lease assistance to Saudi Arabia and within two years the United States sent them moneys and goods exceeding thirty million dollars, a King's ransom in the forties.

During the sixties the price of oil was under two dollars per barrel and five countries that controlled over three fourths of the world's exported oil met and formed what we know today as OPEC. The five original countries were: Saudi Arabia, Kuwait, Iraq, Iran, and Venezuela. By 1973, when the Saudis supported Egypt's war on Israel with money to buy Russian military equipment and supplies, the price of oil went up over threefold. The Saudis warned America that to support Israel in the regional war would be very costly, but America bought the Israeli logic that the Saudis were bluffing because they only had one product to sell and their loyalty to other Arabs would not cause them to 'cut off their nose to spite their face'. History proves this logic was wrong and the price of oil has not been the same ever since, and we Americans have paid for this political decision in our pocketbook and in jobs. So upset were the Saudis with America's support of Israel, that the decision was made for them to take total control of their oil interests and the question of the day was how bad would the OPEC countries punish us.

Because the failure of attempted oil embargoes in 1956 and 1967 the Saudis wanted to leave some room for America to come to their senses. So the Saudi plan was to cut back on oil a percentage each month to any country helping the Israelis, but not to decrease the oil to countries supporting their cause. This is called hardball and the strategy worked for OPEC, with them controlling both the price and who would get the oil. ARAMCO, formed in 1948 by Standard Oil of California, Standard Oil of New Jersey, Texaco, and Mobil, were very worried and expressed their concern directly to then President Nixon, that continuing our aid to Israel would negatively impact their relations with the Saudis.

The timing of this momentous event could not have been worse. For President Nixon the Watergate tapes were being delivered and his day to day activities were for personal survival. To the Department of State fell the responsibility of solving this crisis. A biased American media added fuel to the fire. Even more fuel was added when President Nixon sent to Congress a request for almost three times the money requested by the Israelis. The question that was often floated was, did the President believe he could buy the media and the members of Congress with such a huge amount and wash away his personal problems?

America made her point and with it they lost Saudi Arabia as a friend and gained many enemies that have made Americans pay every day since. Just another day in Washington where those in power do whatever it takes to stay in power no matter what it costs the American people. In this case the cost was more than money, for King Faisal of Saudi Arabia declared holy war on America and all oil shipments to the United States were halted. Both Europe and Japan suffered from this event and the price of oil tripled within weeks and the world hasn't been the same since.

In the U.S., in two years our annual price of oil went from four billion to over twenty billion dollars. The oil embargo was to last only five months but the effect it had in every phase of life in America is still with us and privately the Kingdom of Saudi Arabia has not forgotten or forgiven the decisions that were made in 1973.

With the resumption of Saudi oil the U.S., trying to mend some fences, sold modern military equipment and supplies to the Kingdom and promises were made to help build a modern infrastructure. And as the oil prices soared the Saudis went rushing towards a new problem: what to do with more money than the economy could spend! The solution was to keep much of the new wealth out of the country and to increase the amount of money to be spent modernizing the Kingdom. Entrepreneurs from all the world rushed to assist. Fortunes were made daily and as the newness of the modern world replaced the old, the big question became, how do you bring the advantages of new technologies into the country and keep the problems of the late 20th century outside the borders? How do you allow the foreign workers to increase the costs of their doing business to many times the fair price and not be adversely affected by it? And how with this new found wealth do you allow the people to travel outside your restrictive and well structured society to experience the pleasures of the world and then return to the life they had before? I'm reminded of the old World War I song, "How do you keep them down on the farm after they have seen Paris".

It was to this environment that I boarded a plane to Jeddah, Saudi Arabia in 1990, and it was in this environment where I was treated so well that influenced my feelings of respect and confidence in the Saudis when it came to business. Because they had been taken advantage of by the business ethics of the outside world and yet they treated me so well I came to the conclusion that if you treat the Saudis with respect and don't take advantage of them, they in turn will treat you the same way. Have trust and honor and you will be rewarded with trust and honor.

It was with this feeling that I started Phase I of my five-year employment agreement with King Fahd and Minister Al Shair. The results of that agreement and my continuing efforts to be paid for the work I did for them in 1990, 1991 and 1992 is outlined in the following pages. It is my hope that in writing this book I will be able to close this chapter in my life and forget and forgive the Saudis for their part in it. But the lessons I learned from the United States State Department and the lack of empathy and help from members of Congress will not be forgotten. And this proud American will do all he can to help bring the representative government that democracy promises back to the people. This book is a start in that direction.

PREFACE

In the world I grew up in there was honor and trust. So what happens when an American consultant agrees to create a public relations project for the King and the Minister of Information from the Kingdom of Saudi Arabia and doesn't get paid for his work? This book will answer that question and will detail the journey from the first phone call right up to the last minute.

The details will come from the memory of working for over two years, plus from letters, phone calls, meetings, a diplomatic note, a survey from the Saudi Embassy in Washington DC, and much more. All of this will help the reader to understand how easy it was to be so impressed by the scope and importance of such a project that waiting for the agreed upon compensation was a minor inconvenience that soon would be corrected.

Saudi Arabia officials will use the argument that the work was not really authorized as there was no written contract, and all the people who contacted me had no authority to do so. The fact that these people were high profile employees of Saudi Arabia who exercised similar executive decisions on a daily basis didn't mean they had the authority in my case. How convenient! Try this approach the next time you need the plumber by having your wife call him and after the work is done refuse to pay because your wife doesn't have the authority to hire him.

Imagine being invited to the Saudi Arabia Embassy in Washington DC, to have lunch there, be able to do an extensive survey of the Embassy and the people working there, and be permitted to take a restrictive document from the embassy to be used in a proposal requested by the King. Imagine, to be able to do all this, but no one in authority knew anything about it and no one in the embassy had ever heard of me. I was the unknown stranger admitted through all the security and escorted by Saudi officials to do a survey for a proposal requested by the King. Yet no one had ever heard of me. What an impression I made! Because I was so forgettable I decided to write a book just to be remembered. A book that will concentrate its story inside America and will provide the reader with some insight into the environment that was Saudi Arabia prior to the Gulf War.

This story is about one man's search for that guaranteed right of a worker to be compensated for his work and by a man who believes that in a world without laws and justice there is little hope for mankind to survive. And when Truth, Honesty, and Ethics are replaced by Money, Power, and Greed the bright light that is America starts to fade. If we fail to pay even one person for his labor, can there be any doubt that life as we know it is changing and what happens to one man today may happen to others tomorrow and the more permissive we are the more permissive we become.

Understanding what has happened to me in Saudi Arabia and that other businessmen have had similar experiences should send a warning to those Americans that are now rushing to do billions of dollars worth of business in China. One lesson is clear. Don't count on members of Congress and or the State Department to rush to your aid. They have their own careers and agenda to take care of first, and if you are not in the loop, the loop that costs money to be in, don't believe what happened to me is unusual. It was and is just another day in the life of the elite who make the rules that all the rest of us live by, and be reminded that China is not Saudi Arabia. Saudi Arabia is alive and well because American men and women risked, and some gave up their lives, to protect them and allow their way of life to continue. China is an entirely different ball game and America, with all its power, has little control over any of their actions.

This book was not written to serve as a warning to Americans who engage in international trade. There are enough reminders of the casualties of international trade. But what happened to me should be understood by the small business community as a guide to what can and sometime does happen to us. If this message gets through then this work shall serve a useful purpose and Senator John McCain's major point, that those in power only have time for those who help them stay in power will become loud and clear, and who knows, the future that is tomorrow may yet become today in our lifetime.

CHAPTER ONE

The phone rang. It was Dr. Clive Mohammed calling from Jeddah, Saudi Arabia.

After the normal greetings from one friend to another and the inquiries about each other's families Clive stated: "I'm in King Fahd's office on a speaker phone and I want you to create a public relations project for the Kingdom of Saudi Arabia. Plus, in a formal proposal outline how to start this project, the effectiveness of such a project, and the length of time it would take to become effective."

The bluntness and such a cold, direct approach without any prior discussion made it obvious that Clive was under pressure and my answer should be well measured. I stalled for time to find out what was really going on. So I politely declined and offered as reasons: the time it would consume, how busy I was with my present Saudi project, the enormous scope of such a project, the resistance that would come from an unfriendly media, plus other reasons why the project would be difficult for me to approach at this time.

Clive suggested I investigate and he would get back to me with details. This was quickly agreed to and I thanked him for thinking of me and told him I would wait for his call. Before saying good-bye I again expressed my thanks and softened my resistance to being involved because I assumed that Clive had made promises that I was expected to honor, and that this project was of far greater importance than what he could disclose at that time.

The second phone call from Clive came the next evening and he stated he was in the office of His Excellency Ali Al-Shair, the Minister of Information. He informed me that the Minister would be in charge of the project and I would be directly under his employment with all agreements, moneys, and directions coming from his office. He, Clive, would be our connecting link and I would have access to him at all times. He added that the King and the Minister were anxious for me to start this project and would like my commitment at once.

Again I asked for more time and told him that we could speed the process if the King and the Minister would agree on three specific terms: the length of my employment, moneys guaranteed over a

1

specific period of time, and that Clive would stay in the loop and be available to me here in the U.S. if I really needed him. After a short conversation it was agreed Clive would call me the next morning with all the details and at that time I should be prepared to formally announce my agreement. I didn't mention money or offer any comment to suggest that this was a very costly project and that I would have substantial expenses that also should be considered. I suspected that Clive had already made the agreement and I would be well compensated or Clive wouldn't be involved.

The next morning Clive called with the details. My employment would be for a five-year period, he would be involved, and I would be paid in Phase I the same amount he knew I was paid in Puerto Rico as the consultant for that government. Because this phone call was from his private phone, Clive and I had a long discussion on how important this project was for King Fahd and for Saudi Arabia. Little did we know how true these words would be.

The Gulf War was soon to start and the very existence of Saudi Arabia and Kuwait would depend on America and her Armed Forces coming to the rescue.

The conversation ended with a discussion on what I was to do with my current workload. Clive said he was aware of what I was doing and he had brought to the attention of Minister Al-Shair the project he had previously set up for me in Saudi Arabia. He stated that it was OK for me to continue but I should not take on any other consulting jobs for the next five years. Also, when we started Phase II of this project I would be required to spend all my time committed to Saudi Arabia. The compensation for Phase II would be the same as Phase I but I would be paid expenses, housing in Washington DC, and a large bonus each year. The total budget for Phase II had not been discussed in detail and I was not to ever bring it up until King Fahd had approved Phase I. At that time I would be brought to Saudi Arabia and would be able to give my input on what was needed to be successful. I was assured it would be a first class program and after five years I could retire without any money worries because both the King and the Minister understood what sacrifices I was making.

Due to the fact that Dr. Clive Mohammed, months earlier, had already involved me in what was to be the largest project of my career, it was natural and easy for me to trust that this new venture would be more of the same. Only this time he would be involved.

There was security in that but I still didn't know how he was to be paid and by whom. This was of concern to me because Clive had obviously spent much time to become so involved and had placed his reputation on the line to recommend me so strongly. This was not a casual matter and his employment to the King would certainly be negatively impacted if I didn't perform at a high level and with complete integrity. The fact that Clive was willing to risk so much increased the importance of what I was to do and I was starting to have second thoughts about my decision. But it was too late to say no. It was probably too late to say no before the first phone call, for Clive never did anything without thinking it through. So I would accept his judgment of my abilities and trust he hadn't overestimated me.

CHAPTER TWO

Dr. Clive I. Mohammed, a very articulate, quiet, soft spoken gentleman with perfect manners, was always much more than what you saw and what you knew.

A Pakistani born in Trinidad, he attended several universities and earned D.D.S., M.S., and PH.D degrees. He was a professor in several universities in at least three different countries, who founded one dental school and was a Dean in two other dental schools. Clive was a man of the world who was used to being in the company of high profile, very powerful and successful people. Yet this well educated, highly motivated and hard working man never was able to attain the economic level of those around him. I personally never met anyone with so much talent, who worked so hard with so many projects going on, and failed to accomplish his goals. There was, in my eyes, no one who prepared so well, performed so many tasks at the highest level and was involved in so many different and varied enterprises, who was still not satisfied with his results. He deserved much better than what he received.

Not only, when I met him, was he Chief of Dental Services for the King Fahd Armed Forces Hospital in Jeddah, Saudi Arabia, but he also was the developer of a toothpaste, named Dr. Clive's Fluoroswak, which he marketed outside the U.S. He was a world class professional, the personal dentist for King Fahd as well as several ministers and members of the Royal Family, and other high profile Saudis. Acquainted with many of the 'Right' people in Saudi Arabia, he was the frequent guest at social functions in this country. He sailed on the King's yacht and flew in the King's airplane. It would be fair to say that if there was one American you wanted to know in Saudi Arabia, Dr. Clive I. Mohammed was at the head of the list. He was unique in many ways and a perfect fit as an intelligent, well educated entrepreneur who understood the Arabic language, the religion, and the Saudi way of life. His relationships with successful Western businessmen made him the ideal person to be in Saudi Arabia in the eighties and the nineties. Clive's knowledge, contacts, business experiences and background were just right for a country that was pushing so hard and so fast to catch up with the industrialized countries of the world. They needed more people like Clive and therefore his advice was often sought and the people he recommended for the many opportunities that were so prevalent were well considered.

This I knew personally because in 1989 he had recommended me to a Saudi businessman who soon became my partner. A trip was arranged and I traveled to Jeddah to meet him and worked there calling on Saudi businesses. Each call was well prearranged and I had a letter of introduction from my partner, personalized to the top executive for each business, that outlined the specific topics I would be discussing and the benefits of doing business with us. Each morning I was picked up by one of my partner's sons, driven to each appointment, and introduced to the Saudi in charge of that business. After much tea drinking I was directed down the 'executive line', introduced by the CEO, and finally met the person who was responsible for the specific I was there to talk about. It was not business as usual for this American, but it was a wonderful change for all business was done among friends who knew each other and there existed a bond of trust that included me, for I was not a stranger but a partner of one of their own.

It should be stated that I was most fortunate in Clive's selection of a partner for me, as the man he set me up with became more than a business associate. We became friends and his sons became family to me. As a guest in their home I was treated like one of the family and when the Gulf War started I invited his youngest son and daughter to come live with my family so they would be out of harm's way.

As to my partner, he was well established and anticipated doing hundreds of millions of dollars worth of business in the first year if I could ship all his orders. I did actually ship, successfully, equipment to the Royal Saudi Navy and they were so impressed by my performance that they awarded my partner a contract as one of two contractors that were to supply all the replacement equipment and supplies needed by them. I was faxed an enormous shopping list of the equipment and supplies needed and given a time limit to reply on when I could ship each item. Thanks to the Governor of Maryland at that time, who had set up an international division to serve Maryland businesses and had heard of me, I was able to secure delivery dates on every item but one on this long list. Our celebration was cut short as my friend and partner died very suddenly and unexpectedly, and by

Saudi law a non-Saudi cannot do business in Saudi Arabia without a Saudi partner. Although Clive could find me another partner, I declined and put all my energies into the King's project to make Saudi Arabia's Public Relations Project the best effort I was capable of doing. It seemed to me that in this way I could also keep in contact with the Saudis I had met and who had treated me so well. I was anxious to return to the Saudi Arabia I had experienced, not knowing that what was about to happen to me would change the way I felt about doing business there.

CHAPTER THREE

The Public Relations Project I did for the Kingdom of Saudi Arabia is very complex and the names of the major players are not familiar to most Americans. To make it easier for the reader to better understand the work I did and why I felt so secure in working for thirty-one months without being paid the agreed upon compensation, allow me to introduce the eight most prominent people involved and detail a few of the most notable events that took place from 1990 to 1997.

- King Fahd- King of Saudi Arabia since 1982.
- Prince Bandar bin Sultan- Ambassador of Saudi Embassy, Washington D.C.
- Adel Al-Jubeir- First Secretary, Saudi Embassy and assistant to His Royal Highness Prince Bandar.
- Abdulrahman Al-Shaia- Second Secretary, Saudi Embassy, Washington, D.C.
- Sheikh Ali Al-Shair- Minister of Information and close friend to King Fahd.
- Dr. Soraya Al-Mashat- Employee of Minister Al-Shair sent by him to work in the Saudi Embassy and report to him on her mission in Washington.
- Dr. Clive Mohammed- Chapter Two
- Professor and Attorney Joseph Siracusa- Attorney at Law in private practice for over forty years and professor of law at a local college. All faxes, correspondences, and many of the daily phone calls originated at his office where I also had an office that I attended to at least five days of the week. He also accompanied me on trips, the most notable being the four-day meetings with Dr. Clive Mohammed in Sarasota, Florida.

In early 1990 after three phone calls, I started Phase I of a two-phase public relations project for the Kingdom of Saudi Arabia. Phase I was to create a public relations project that would change the way most Americans think of Arabs in general, and the Saudis in

7

particular. I was to daily monitor news media, do research, analyze the news, and show the technique to put the Arabs' best foot forward without creating a negative response. I sent print media to Dr. Mohammed on a continual basis, and articles from Saudi, which were printed in English, were sent or faxed to me.

Within Phase I, I was to create a formal proposal that would outline:

- How to start the project
- Effectiveness of the project
- Time it would take to become effective
- Explain in detail how I would respond to major news items that would relate to the Kingdom or items that the Kingdom would have an educational or economic interest in

I worked on Phase I for over thirty-one months. The money was always being sent, 'the check is in the mail' syndrome. The months passed quickly as I worked twelve to sixteen hour days and progress towards the start of Phase II continued at a positive pace. The major events that kept my attitude positive and my daily work habits on a high level was the anticipation of the start of Phase II, where I would begin the public relations project setting up my first office in Washington, D.C.

During July, August, September and October of 1990 I daily worked on the project and on October 19, 1990, Clive called and stated, "Minister Al-Shair formally approved the project but King Fahd needs more information". Twelve days later, on October 31, 1990, Clive called very excited and wanted me to send him a general outline of the proposal. I quickly created the outline and it was immediately typed and faxed from my attorney's office.

Clive called on November 27, 1990 with instructions for me to fax my reply, that "I was ready to come to Saudi Arabia to meet both King Fahd and Minister Al-Shair". The King wanted to have meetings with me and get to know me personally. This was very important as it would speed up the start of Phase II and I would have the pleasure of meeting the King and his Minister of Information. I was excited and proud that a person from my social economic beginnings could have such an opportunity. Could this be another American success story? Surely one to tell my children and grandchildren about.

In December 1990, Clive set up meetings for both my attorney and me to meet him at his wife's house in Sarasota, Florida so we could have private conversations away from interruptions. During these meetings on January 11, 12, 13 and 14 the key elements stressed were:

- The secrecy of Phase I
- How the Gulf War was changing attitudes and priorities
- The problems of American troops inside Saudi Arabia
- The need for me to anticipate problems if the war lasted much longer, and to supply a list of possible public relation solutions to each problem that might occur (e.g. Ramadan and Hajj with hundreds of thousands of infidel troops fighting near the two most holy cities.)

On January 13, 1991 Clive reached by phone his Excellency Ali Al-Shair, went over our discussions the past two days and with Clive, Irma Mohammed and Attorney Siracusa listening to the conversation, Clive handed the phone to me. The Minister expressed his thanks and confidence in me and my work. He listened to my views on the need to start Phase II at once, because the climate would never be better for America to embrace her Saudi partner and start the process to understand the difference in custom, dress, and modernity were not obstacles. No sooner did I express my view when he stated, "Give your passport data to Dr. Clive and we will have you on a plane to come meet the King on January 17, 1991. Dr. Clive will accompany you and we will start the project at once." I agreed but offered the observation that four days was a short time to get my passport in order. He suggested that between him and the King this would not be a problem. After hanging up the phone, being embarrassed by my friends on my naivety, we enjoyed a victory celebration before getting back to the seriousness of the business at hand. The next day my attorney and I flew back to Syracuse, with my attorney trying to figure out how he could accompany me on this historic trip. Unfortunately he was not invited and I would again go to Saudi Arabia alone.

The trip was delayed when the Gulf War escalated. Twelve days later, on January 25, 1991, Second Secretary Abdulrahman A. Al-Shaia of the Royal Embassy of Saudi Arabia in Washington, D.C. called to inform me that Minister of Information Ali Al-Shair had contacted the Embassy and I was to with great haste, finish my formal proposal and deliver it to him personally at the embassy so he could forward it to the Minister by diplomatic carrier.

The Second Secretary and I talked several times with each conversation ending with him telling me of the urgency of this project. On January 28, 1991 I was told to be at the Saudi Embassy on February 6, 1991 with the complete proposal. Clive called the next day and instructed me to stop all contact with the Embassy, and he would fly to Washington to meet with me on February 5, 1991 and fill me in on what was going on. My questions about the purpose of this trip and why that specific date were not answered. I knew then that there was much more to the project than I was being told and suspected that the work I was doing for King Fahd was not an open project and the 'need to know' approach was in place. I wondered how much I knew and when I would be in the 'inner circle'.

It was now more important that my proposal would show my competence and my knowledge, so I invited public relation experts to review my work. After three meetings it was agreed that my proposal was excellent even though I was totally opposed to a conventional huge, high cost media blitz to start the program. I was still not satisfied and took my proposal to be reviewed by an executive of a large prestigious public relations agency. It was graded outstanding and a price tag of one million dollars was placed on it with five hundred thousand to be paid up front. I was told that the fair market value for my work was only five hundred thousand, but for Saudi Arabia it was best to double the price and receive full value up front in case I wasn't paid. I quickly dismissed this logic because of my experience when in Saudi Arabia, where my problem was in refusing to accept money before the work was done. I could not imagine that the King of such a wealthy country that had solicited my services would not honor the agreement that Clive had crafted. I was sure it was money in the bank.

On February 5, 1991 I drove early into Washington and met with my aid from a past project in another country, and had him drive me to my appointment with Clive. Attorney Siracusa had strongly advised me that I should have a local presence that was well acquainted with the Washington scene. It was fortunate I did because my meeting with Clive was in a hotel lobby, not a room, and was very short. With little intrigue he explained to me that he was staying at a highly secure multi-million dollar apartment of a senior vice-president of Mobil Oil where we could have total privacy. Plus, he had invited an employee of Minister Al-Shair to join us.

My aid was dismissed and we took a cab to where Clive was staying. After a short conversation, Clive made a phone call and we were joined by Dr. Soraya Al-Mashat, who also lived in this building and who was a long time trusted employee of Minister Al-Shair. Dr. Al-Mashat was the Advisor in the Information Office of the Royal Embassy of Saudi Arabia in Washington. After many hours of going through my proposal and explaining my plans, I was congratulated on my work and told, "This proposal cannot be reviewed by anyone in the Embassy and I should cancel my appointment." When I strongly objected, very explicit reasons were given on why the Embassy could not see my proposal, or even know that it was a completed work. Dr. Clive explained the reasons why he was instructed by Minister Al-Shair to fly to Washington for the meeting and that he was to hand carry the proposal directly to a meeting with King Fahd and Minister Al-Shair.

I convinced Dr. Clive and Dr. Mashat that I was determined to go to my meeting as planned and both of them could accompany me. Dr. Mashat returned to her residence, and Clive and I had long discussions over many issues, money being high on the list. It was finally decided that the meeting would go as planned and Clive would get approval for five hundred thousand dollars for my proposal before I released it, and all monies owed to that date would be sent immediately after Clive delivered the proposal.

The next day, Dr. Clive and I went to the Embassy where Dr. Mashat met us. We were guests of Dr. Mashat's at lunch and then the three of us went to my one o'clock meeting with the Second Secretary. At the meeting, I informed the Second Secretary that I needed to do a survey of the Embassy to complete my proposal and that King Fahd had requested that Clive hand-carry the proposal to him and Minister Al-Shair. The meeting lasted a couple of hours and ended when the Second Secretary asked me, "Who is compensating you for this trip and the proposal?" Clive immediately replied, "Mr.

Dickson is on a five-year agreement with the King and all monies are being paid out of the Minister of Information Office." Before we left his office, the Second Secretary asked Dr. Mashat to take me on a tour of the Embassy and report back to him after the tour.

The tour of the Embassy was highlighted when I talked to several young male American college graduates whose job was to monitor all media news programs, and twice-per-day news releases were created for review by select personnel of the Embassy. The daily news summary of February 6, 1991, 10 a.m. edition, was given to me to be part of my proposal. This discovery was very important to me because it would save me at least three people for my project and I would finally have a local, high profile person to work with.

This very important restricted document is printed here to give validity to the importance the Saudi Embassy placed on me and the King's Public Relations Project, and to take a look back in history on what was the News of the Day at this critical point of the Gulf War. Little did we realize that eleven years later the problem of Iraq and Saddam Hussein would be revisited.

ROYAL EMBASSY OF SAUDI ARABIA
INFORMATION OFFICE
WASHINGTON, D.C.

DAILY NEWS SUMMARY   **10 AM EDITION**   **FEBRUARY 6, 1991**

- **N.Y. Times:** Heavy allied bombing has not substantially weakened combat effectiveness of Iraq's Republican Guards.

- **UPI:** Ground assault is near as warplanes switch from conventional bombs to more precise Maverick missiles.

- **W.S. Journal:** Bush believes ground war will be necessary, intelligence reports suggest Iraqi military crumblling.

SAUDI ARABIA

SAUDIS IN QUANDARY OVER HAJJ

David Zucchino, Miami Herald (Knight-Ridder): "Saudis in Quandary Over Annual Pilgrimage" (Washington) — Saudi Arabia is on the brink of a decision that could risk its standing in the Arab world even more than the one that allowed a half-million "infidel" US troops into the homeland of Islam's two holiest sites.

"The Hajj is causing the Saudis some very big problems. It's a real paradox for them," said Nubar Hovsepian, a professor of Middle East politics at Hunter College in New York. According to Hovsepian and other Muslim scholars, the Saudis pushed for a January attack by the US-led forces in hopes of ending the war before the hajj. But now that American leaders are describing a war that could last for months, the Saudis are delaying their usual announcements of hajj preparations. Scholars predict that the Saudis will use the war as a reason to enforce strict quotas. (11-A) [NAA]

13

James L. Dickson Jr.

OPERATION DESERT STORM

EFFECTIVENESS OF BOMBING OF REPUBLICAN GUARDS DISPUTED

Patrick Tyler, N.Y. Times: "Best Iraqi Troops Not Badly Hurt by Bombs, Pentagon Officials Say" (Washington) -- Pentagon officials said Tuesday that after nearly three weeks of heavy bombing, the US and allied military forces in the Arabian Gulf have not substantially weakened the combat effectiveness of Iraq's elite ground forces in a well-entrenched "strategic reserve" in Northern Kuwait and southern Iraq. The officials say that the strategic reserve, about 10 divisions of crack Republican Guards and Army tank units, is substantially intact with well-dispersed underground depots and supply lines despite the daily pounding from allied air forces.

Tank and artillery losses are in the "low hundreds," the officials said, and up to six months' worth of supplies have been salted away in thousands of small depots that cannot be targeted by allied bombers. One military official with access to detailed bomb damage assessment information from the war zone said of President Saddam Hussein: "By my personal estimate, in spite of the massive interdiction campaign, we have not reduced his ability to supply his theater forces below his rate of consuming those supplies. So it has not been necessary for him to start feeling on his in-place stocks."

"It is still, substantially, the fighting it was," the official said. "And I have every reason to believe that the Republican Guard can still be employed as an effective fighting force and it has not yet been substantially degraded. That is not to say air power has failed, but there is still a lot of work to do." The official said "nobody in his right mind" in the military hierarchy believes that allied forces have cut the fighting capability of Saddam Hussein's forces in half.

The assessment does not mean that the effectiveness of the Republican Guards is totally unimpaired or that the air campaign has been without military benefit to the allies. The Iraqi air force has been damaged significantly, meaning that when the Republican Guards come out of fortified positions to fight, they will be exposed by their lack of air cover, but will retain close-in antiaircraft capabilities.

The assessment rates fighting strength based on several criteria: maneuverability, fire support, air defense, intelligence and electronic warfare, mobility and counter-mobility, survivability and sustainment.

"I don't think we've started to degrade the maneuver capability of the Republican Guards," a military official said. "That's the hard work of killing tanks and we are in a low hundreds, but he has got 5,000." In fire support, allied forces have been attacking Iraq's 160 artillery battalions with mixed success. "The B-52's are not doing too well because the dispersal pattern" of Iraq's artillery and armor "is too great" for the

---

14

"area explosions" of the high-altitude bombers. the official said. Simple sand bags and sand resentments also cut down the effectiveness of both conventional and cluster bombs. (A-1) [NAA]

AIR FORCE SWITCH TO MAVERICK MISSILES SIGNALS GROUND WAR IS NEAR

United Press International: "US missile Switch May Signal Ground War" (Saudi Arabia) -- US fighter-bomber pilots have switched from conventional bombs to more precise Maverick missiles - a move seen as a possible indication of final preparations for a ground assault in the Gulf war.

"It tells me a few days down the road they're (ground troops) going to me moved," Air Force Sgt. Richard Bradly said at a base in central Saudi Arabia where the Mavericks were being loaded onto jets for the first time Tuesday. [NAA]

BUSH BELIEVES GROUND WAR WILL BE NECESSARY

Gerald Seib and Andy Pasztor. W.S. Journal: "Bush Is Skeptical Air Strikes Can Free Kuwait From Iraq" (Washington) -- President Bush said he is "somewhat skeptical" that air power alone will force Iraqi troops to leave Kuwait, as new intelligence reports suggest Iraq's ability to resist a ground offensive is diminishing rapidly.

Intelligence reports are indicating that the ferocious air campaign has cut off some Iraqi front-line units from fuel supplies and communications with senior commanders. That might make it easier for Bush to order ground action because Iraqi ability to resist will have been reduced.

At the Pentagon, planners now say that the damage to Iraq's military fuel storage and distribution system is so severe that many of Saddam Hussein's troops in Kuwait wouldn't be able to keep tanks and artillery rolling to counter rapidly moving US armored assaults.

"We have destroyed a very, very significant portion of their refining and storage system, there isn't any question about that," said one high-level Pentagon official who has sat in on the most recent intelligence briefings. "Such targets continue to be among the highest priority."

More important, Pentagon officials said, the aerial bombardment has at least temporarily severed communications between senior Iraqi generals and several of their divisions along the Kuwaiti border. These divisions may be unable to receive timely orders if a ground war errupts. (A-3) [JDH]

US SLOW TO TURN OVER POWs

Peter Ford, C.S. Monitor: "Coalition Forces Slow To Deliver Iraqi POWs To Saudi Hosts" (Dhahran) -- As the Gulf war

James L. Dickson Jr.

DAILY NEWS SUMMARY
10 AM EDITION--WEDNESDAY
FEBRUARY 6, 1991/PAGE 4

continues, the number of Iraqi prisoners of war is mounting. Although accurate figures are impossible to come by, about 1,000 are currently being held, with signs that American units are not always handing their prisoners on as quickly as they are meant to. Asked about the apparent delay in passing the EPWs into Saudi hands, a US military spokeswoman said the time US forces hold the Iraqis just depends on the circumstances of their capture.

US forces are believed to be holding their Iraqi prisoners longer, however, in order to extract intelligence information from them before moving them to the rear. (p.6) [JDH]

GULF CRISIS

SAUDI AL-FAISAL MEETS WITH MUBARAK

Reuters: **"Mubarak Confers With Saudi Foreign Minister"** (Cairo) -- President Hosni Mubarak met Wednesday Saudi Foreign Minister Prince Saudi Al-Faisal to discuss the Arabian Gulf war. Prince Saudi Al-Faisal arrived in Cairo Tuesday night from a Damascus, where he met with President Hafez al-Assad and Syrian Foreign Minister Farouk Sharaa. No details were given on the topics discussed during the meetings. [NAA]

US, BRITAIN PLANNING FOR POST-WAR ERA

Warren Strobel and Martin Sieff, Washington Times: **"US. Britain Begin Planning War's Aftermath"** -- The US and Britain have begun discussing postwar plans for the Middle East that would prevent a repeat of Iraq's invasion of Kuwait, according to officials from both countries.

British and US officials said London has floated what one diplomat called a "very embryonic idea" for a postwar peacekeeping force in the Gulf that would have little, if any, participation from US and British troops. They cover everything from security in the Gulf to the Arab-Israeli dispute and the proliferation of modern weapons in the region. But the planning cannot go much further until a key question is answered: whether Saddam Hussein survives in power.

A British diplomat, speaking on condition of anonymity, said that while there are no "blueprints, no format suggestions" about how to prevent further Middle East wars, it is clear that the GCC needs buttressing.

British Foreign Secretary Douglas Hurd said Saturday in a speech to Conservative Party members that "the Gulf states will want to look at how they can live in a secure peace with their neighbors in Iran and Iraq and at whether there is a role for other Islamic countries slightly further afield - Egypt, Turkey, Syria, Pakistan."

British diplomats in London have suggested that the peacekeeping

---
Please do not reproduce or distribute this material.
It is intended for your own use only

16

DAILY NEWS SUMMARY
10 AM EDITION--WEDNESDAY
FEBRUARY 6, 1991/PAGE 5

force could be led by Egypt and might be based in Bahrain. The peacekeeping force would have at the most a minimal US and British presence in order not to provoke an anti-Western reaction in the Arab world and without "putting the clock back," as Hurt said in the speech. (A-8) [NAA]

ARAB-AMERICANS

MAJORITY OF ARAB-AMERICANS SUPPORT WAR EFFORT

Mimi Hall, USA Today: "Poll: Most Support US In Gulf War" -- Two-thirds of Arab-Americans support the US war effort as combat enters a fourth week, and see a genuine need to stop Saddam Hussein. But despite the support for the troops in the Gulf, the Arab-American community is deeply divided by the massive bombing of Iraq.

Nearly all say Iraq should get out of Kuwait, most support President Bush and think the US needs to support its Arab allies. But the degree of support hinges on whether those questioned were Christian or Muslim, whether they are US-born or immigrants. Of the 501 Arab-Americans polled, 70% were Christian, 30% were Muslim; 77% of the Christians support the war, 36% of the Muslims do. (A-1) [JDH]

EGYPT

MAJOR UNREST IS FEARED IN EGYPT IF WAR LASTS INTO SPRING

Jane Mayer, W.S. Journal: "Egypt Braces for Pro-Iraqi Shift at Home" (Cairo) -- As the war in the Gulf continues, the small and fragmented opposition to Egypt's government gains focus and strength, causing concern that, should the war last into the spring, the political climate could become volatile. Egyptians warn that if the war is still gong strong in March, during Ramadan, public opinion in Egypt will grow increasingly pro-Iraqi.

"The government doesn't see its support slipping in the street right now," is the way one Western diplomat in Cairo puts it, "but they are more worried about the long term. We all are."

There is widespread doubt that there will be massive pro-Iraqi demonstration in Egypt or that the opposition will try using violence to change the government position. But nonetheless, the government has been cracking down on opposition leaders who have been speaking out against the pro-West stance Mubarak has expressed during the conflict. (A-8) [JDH]

17

James L. Dickson Jr.

DAILY NEWS SUMMARY
10 AM EDITION--WEDNESDAY
FEBRUARY 6, 1991/PAGE 6

MAGREB

NORTH AFRICAN COUNTRIES CHURNING OVER GULF WAR

Steve Greenhouse, N.Y. Times: "War Puts Strain On North Africa" (Tunis) -- The Gulf war is causing great strains on the Governments of Tunisia, Algeria and Morocco, which face intense public pressure to back Iraq but also fear angering Western nations. Bowing to public pressure, North African leaders have started to condemn the US-led offensive against Iraq, while through private diplomatic channels they are asking Western governments to understand their plight.

North African officials say one reason they called for a United Nations cease-fire in January was that they wanted the war to end as soon as possible to help extricate them from their delicate sittuation. Those officials were quick to add that they also want a cease-fire to save the Iraqis from further pummeling by the American-led attacks. (A-11) [JDH]

NEWSBRIEFS

(Reuters) -- Israeli police said Wednesday they arrested two more Israeli Arabs suspected of belonging to a pro-Iraqi spy ring, bringing to 12 the number of arrested in the past two weeks... [NAA]

(Reuters) -- A knife-wielding Palestinian wounded an Israeli soldier on a bus Wednesday in the first such incident since the Gulf war began, security sources said... [NAA]

(Reuters) -- Dr. Ruth says the threat of an Iraqi gas attack is bound to take its toll on Israeli couples... [NAA]

(AP) -- Forty kuwaitis are volunteering to serve as guides and interpreters for British troops in the Gulf war, the British Ministry of Defense said... [NAA]

(Reuters) -- France said Tuesday it had gained agreement from EC governments for gas masks to be sent to Palestinians in Israeli-occupied territories... [NAA]

* * * * * * * *

Please do not reproduce or distribute this material.
It is intended for your own use only

18

Unfortunately, the idea of having a local high profile person from the Saudi Washington Embassy was soundly rejected, and I was told not to have any future contact with the Embassy, with the exception of Dr. Mashat, as she was an employee of Minister Al-Shair. The reasons were confidential, and I did not completely understand the politics until late 1997. As I had enough on my plate to do in a short period of time, I concentrated on my job and left the politics to the professionals. Before saying goodbye, Clive took me to the waterfront and we went aboard his Mobil Oil friend's large cruiser. The hour aboard this beautiful ship gave me a total expanded view of who Clive was, and what he wanted from life.

Time passed very quickly. The phone and fax bills, my expenses, and the lack of income were becoming an issue. On March 11, 1991 King Fahd approved the contract and Dr. Clive went over budget details including:

- $500,000 for a proposal
- $225,000 for nine months work

Eight days later, on March 19, 1991 there was a meeting between Clive and Minister Al-Shair on my monies and new budget for our office in Washington. The budget included payroll for people, equipment, and my annual salary to be paid up-front each year. I was asked to go to Washington and confirm office and equipment costs, plus interview people that were needed. This I did on April 8, 1991.

King Fahd brought up a new challenge. He would not proceed to Phase II until three questions were answered to his satisfaction. On May 6, 1991 I had completed my answers to King Fahd's questions:

- Question—How to insure that the project would not produce negative results.

Answer—Avoid using any advertising/public relations corporations with their high profile, highly charged media blitzes:

1. Creative media blitz procedures produce instant opinions with the fallout going in many directions and results cannot be predicted with a high degree of accuracy.

2. Cannot control material even with oversight.
3. Public opinions can change on a dime; the wrong word or phrase can increase or decrease poll numbers among a wide variety of the American public.

- Question—How to keep control

Answer—have a low-key, long-range conservative program with all new material cleared by Minister Al-Shair but still retain the ability to respond to negative media perceptions on a real time basis.

- Question—Size of operation, start and future

Answer—Start in Washington and work slowly through major select cities.

1. First office expansion in Syracuse where I already had an office and availability of a highly trained professional group of people.
2. Expand where large populations of Arabs reside.
3. Maps and pages with populations for each site were enclosed.

On July 26, 1991 I sent a special delivery letter to Dr. Clive for delivery to Minister Al-Shair. In this letter, I asked for an exact start-up date and when I could expect payment. I could not fax due to security. The reply to this letter was that King Fahd is delaying the start of Phase II as the Embassy has not been in the loop and it will take time to work this out. I should continue monitoring the media daily and send all related articles with my solutions on how to respond to each event. Plus, keep Dr. Clive up to date by expanding the proposal to keep it current.

Again I asked for payment of monies owed and again the same replies that the monies owed were like money in the bank and the difficulty was not economic or any way related to a budget consideration. The problem they had to work out was the 'accounting vehicle' they would use to keep this project out of the mainstream until they were ready to announce it. I was told that this was an internal problem, a policy that had to be worked out by King Fahd personally. Disappointed, but with so much at stake, money and time, I was left with little choice but to play the hand dealt to me, suck it up, and keep positive.

For the next six months I kept working the plan and enlarging the proposal. Finally in the summer of 1992 I stopped working on the project and all contact with Clive was about money, with my last contact with him on February 19, 1996 with Clive calling me to do a 'special' project for him personally. He asked me at this time if I had received all the monies owed as Minister Al-Shair had promised him in the summer of 1995 that he was starting to send me $100, 000.00 per month until all monies owed were paid. In this way they could hide that I had been employed for a project that was not going forward. Feeling abused, I took my story outside the Kingdom of Saudi Arabia.

I started in 1997 to tell my story to select individuals that I hoped would support my efforts to be paid, and who could take my case directly to the Saudis. My first effort was an anchor for one of the major networks and it was suggested that I should allow them to investigate the validity of my claims and if they were satisfied, they would 'air' my story on one of their weekly national shows. I rejected this idea because once the media takes over, total control is in their hands and the direction and duration of time given to any story is dictated by ratings and how well the story is received.

The more people I talked to, the less optimistic I felt. People do things for their own reasons and the solution to my problem would only help the Dickson family. Discouraged, but not ready to throw in the towel, I asked myself a simple question. Where do you go for help on an international business dispute? If it is with Saudi Arabia, the court system cannot help unless there is an asset in the United States. There are many cases that prove this point, and several of them are - found locally in Syracuse, NY. Another case, quoting from an article in a Florida paper stated, "Saks sues Saudi Prince to recoup $720, 673. Saks Fifth Avenue says a Saudi Arabian Prince is overdue in paying $720, 673 in charge card purchases. Prince Abdullah bin Faisal bin Abdulaziz made the purchases from 1997 to July 1999 at a Saks in Bal Harbour, Florida, according to a law suit filed Tuesday in state circuit court. The company hasn't received a payment since April 1999, Saks lawyer Scott Chapman said. The outstanding balance on the Prince's account topped $1.9 million after a May 2,

James L. Dickson Jr.

1998 buying spree that totaled $1.5 million, Chapman said. The lawsuit was filed in West Palm Beach, Florida, because the Prince owns commercial property worth an estimated $6 million there."

This lawsuit failed and was finally dropped by Saks Fifth Avenue. Again, as in my case, economics was not the problem. If Saks cannot collect a charge card debt, what chance does a small businessman have of even 'playing the game'? The answer, of course, is none. So if going to the courts in the U.S. is not the answer, how about following the advice of the American Ambassador to Saudi Arabia. His suggestion was to hire a Saudi attorney and sue in Saudi Arabia. If there is anyone out there that believes this is a solution, please call, and I have a piece of the Brooklyn Bridge that I'll sell you cheap.

You can't go to court, how about help from a member of Congress? Isn't this one of their prime duties? It certainly is one of their most notable promises when election time comes around. Most of us understand that politics and money interfere with the good judgment of our elected officials. After all, elections are won with money and not with good ideas. The people without the price of admission, you and me, don't have a seat at the table. We understand, not really, that some Americans are more equal than others. Remember, it only takes money to get you a 'seat at the table', and if you make a large enough contribution, you may be one of the lucky few to have a member of Congress actually remember your name and even invite you to a party where you can again advance the cause of democracy and contribute more money to help assure his or her election.

Although I was not one of the 'lucky few' to actually be invited to one of their parties, I was invited into the three senate offices and did have a personal meeting with my Congressman at his Utica office. At each of the Senators offices, I was on a time restraint and asked to quickly explain why I wanted to take up their time. I felt like a poor beggar going from one member of Congress to another, but it was the only option that was open to me.

CHAPTER FOUR

I have been told by many people who have taken an interest in my writing that I should include my proposal in this book. I was reluctant to even consider it at first, for it was difficult for me to release even a portion of the ideas I thought were important over a decade ago when America was at war. This was a different war than Americans were used to and the way it would end has come to affect us past today's reality. But with so many of the people who's judgment was so important to me advising in the same voice, I decided to read once more this work I spent so much time doing that was so well received by all who read it.

After reading the proposal I agreed that it would give the reader an insight as to the scope and importance of this project, and would help to explain what I proposed to do and show how dedicated I was to this assignment. It would also very closely point out that the Kingdom of Saudi Arabia very much needed to do a Public Relations Project in the 1990's, and if they had, the entire Middle East Region could have benefited. Many of the ideas I stressed are now being stressed by the Saudis, and many of the problems I feared might occur have in fact surfaced. You will find examples of both the ideas stressed and the problems that I thought might occur after the Gulf War ended in the excerpts of the proposal contained in this chapter.

Creating proposals for my consulting services are a normal activity and over the last twenty-five years I have written proposals on many subjects for a wide variety of clients. One proposal was over a hundred pages with many copies, and done with a hard cover in book form to be used to perform the function it was written to create. Because Dr. Clive was familiar with this particular project he had recommended to both King Fahd and the Minister that a formal proposal was needed.

There were several reasons why I was asked to create a formal proposal. This was a huge, expensive and critical project the King and the Minister wanted me to do, and what better way to find out if I was capable, than to have me prepare a proposal for them to evaluate. They could compare my approach to the twenty plus proposals created by the largest Advertising/Public Relations Corporations that

James L. Dickson Jr.

were presented to Prince Bandar and First Secretary Adel Al-Jubeir, and if I was found lacking they could stop the project before it started. The fact I knew nothing about this competition until late 1997 was a good indication I was not yet 'in the loop'.

My approach was to create a written work that was not a strict structured method to follow on all occasion, rather a guide to the boundaries where individual views could be expressed and change could be implemented to keep up with the fast pace of the ever changing world. You can take turns in the road but never change the direction of keeping the Saudi philosophy and way of life as the bright light to guide you. We would use the principle that the founding father, King Abdul, used when he created the Kingdom but also takes advantage of the progress in modern technology, health care, methods of travel, etc.

My proposal was a road to follow, a track to run on. It would be a work in progress that we would add to, change, but always within the guide lines of our overall philosophy of keeping the Saudis way of life as the foundation to build upon, and slowly allow America to see the Saudis as they really are and not as depicted by a biased media.

In the years that followed my proposal the Saudis have tried on several occasions to create a Public Relations Project by using conventional corporate advertising methods. In my opinion, each attempt has failed, and it was rumored that in the Spring of 2002 their approach was turned down by Public Relations Corporations who were reluctant to take their business and print their messages. Could this have possibly happened? I warned them about an unfriendly media in my proposal, which was presented to King Fahd and the Minister of Information Ali Al-Shair in February 1991. As you will read, this was not the only activity I was concerned about, but it is my 'guess' that the proposal stayed with Minister Al-Shair and was never made available so the Minister could 'hide' that I was ever employed by the Kingdom of Saudi Arabia.

Here are the excerpts from the proposal that was hand carried to King Fahd and Minister Al-Shair by Dr. Clive Mohammed in February 1991.

PROPOSAL

CONSULTANT/ PUBLIC RELATIONS

FOR

SAUDI ARABIA

J. L. DICKSON
ASSOCIATES

25

INTRODUCTION

I.   This proposal is an outline of objectives and the methods to achieve these objectives. Volumes could be written about each topic and the various ways to proceed, but as events unfold and new problems are confronted in an ever changing environment, the key to success is in the ability to be both flexible to adjust to today's needs and to be consistent in the messages that you desire to promote.

Although one changes to adapt to the news of today and the new challenges that occur, your message does not vary. The bottom line is always the same. Simply stated, keep up with the times, but never change the focus of the project. For what is important in today's news is not popular tomorrow. The media creates importance to events they report and the public chases the illusion, but the philosophy of a country and the achievements of its people are recorded in history and the way that history is presented to the people of the world creates the image that the world has forever.

It is to this end that this project is dedicated: to help the people "see" the Arab in general and the Saudi in particular as a positive reflection of the world's values. Different customs and unfamiliar dress are not a negative but merely minor obstacles to understanding. The goal is the same for all people, only the means to that end are different.

II.   It has become critical to prepare for the Post War World. It is possible to win the war and lose the peace. The Arab world will be changed, possibly fragmented, and the Saudi can be in harm's way in the fall out if we do not prepare now. We must build an image and build a relationship with America and its people. The Gulf area will change and a new power structure will emerge to become the dominant player in the area. This player should have the support of the American people as well as it's government if it is to succeed.

We will start to build an image toward this end. To become the moderate, peaceful friend and ally of America, with opportunities for both countries to prosper economically and politically in their march to bring real lasting peace and freedom to all the people of the region. It is time that the dominant player in the Gulf be the country that has no plans for expansion of her borders and is economically strong enough to bring about reforms that will insure the area's growth in an ever expanding world.

III. It is hoped that this project will grow from a very modest and conservative effort to become a permanent and important way to bring the people of Saudi Arabia and America to a better understanding of each other. Additionally, we will work together in a relationship as partners to help make this a better world for all people to live in peace, prosperity and without fear.

IV. It should be pointed out that there is 'overlapping' from one objective to another. Although it is not intentional, this is natural if we are to achieve our goal of educating the U.S. population as to the desired image of the average Saudi citizen. As we proceed, we will find that each objective will overlap until finally we have developed the complete image of the modern Saudi in the 1990's. We must always maintain this focus in each objective.

V. Finally, one of our methods in utilizing Public Relations Techniques is to strategically alter and/or clarify the public's conception of Saudi Arabia and its people. By first understanding the public view Americans have, then by establishing the Saudi point of view, we will change public opinion to arrive at our goal.

27

<u>OBJECTIVE I</u>

SET UP AND MAINTAIN THE VARIOUS LEVELS OF PUBLIC RELATIONS CAMPAIGN FOR THE SAUDI ARABIAN WAY OF LIFE. FACT VS. FICTION.

AREAS OF OPPORTUNITY ARE:

A. Use positive imaging by depicting the crime and drug free society of Saudi Arabia, where people can walk the streets safely 24 hours a day.

B. Publish pictures of the modern cities and shopping centers that show people buying the same products purchased in America and driving the same cars.

C. Show the modern hospitals and dental facilities with the world's latest state of the arts equipment and procedures, provided by the best doctors and dentists in the world, with many coming from America and the Western World. Computers at every nursing station plus the modern pneumatic tube systems provide accurate patient data and a fast system of internal transportation for testing, lab procedures, etc.

D. Compare educational systems and show similarities of subjects studied and methods of teaching, where students learn in both Arabic and English. At the high school level many are sent to private schools outside the country and a high percentage attend American Colleges.

E. Compare the phone system, mass transportation and government created and maintained public works as well as modern communications, new highways and government parks for the people's leisure time. Feature the all modern, government created and maintained desalination plant.

28

F. Keep in focus the Saudi and United States agreement to maintain the Saudi "way of life" for the American troops in the desert. Publicize the United States findings that the American fighting force has a higher rate of efficiency in the desert than anywhere else in the world. This reported fact was attributed to the no drinking rule encouraged by the Saudis.

G. Counter negative statements and campaigns by groups that are harmful to Saudi in particular and Arabs in general.

H. Through all these efforts will be an exemplification of the typical Saudi family, where the family unit is the center of all activities. It is similar to the American family life of the early 20th century with its high moral, ethical, religious and patriotic values.

OBJECTIVE II

CREATE GRASS ROOTS AWARENESS AND SUPPORT IN:

A. Local Arab/American organizations.
    1. Cultural
    2. Civic
    3. Government
B. Educational.
    1. College campuses

C. Government
    1. Local
    2. State
        a. Investment opportunities, similar to the states of Maryland and Virginia.

D. Advertising
    1. Use all media

E. Corporations and their executives
    1. Especially those now doing business in Saudi Arabia.

F. Use key local Arab/Americans as volunteers to build an organization from one area to another.

OBJECTIVE III

CREATE A SAUDI ARABIAN/UNITED SATES INDUSTRIAL SUPPORT GROUP.

A. Multi national corporations and their corporate executives are anxious to exchange ideas and do business with each other.

B. Set up selective state governments with an "expert" on Saudi Arabia.
    1. Work with and train U.S. expert so he is knowledgeable of Saudi products and has the names of Saudi businessmen that he can communicate with when the need occurs.

C. Have seminars on opportunities for business with Saudi Arabia.
    1. This can be expanded to Europe quickly and easily using our business friends in select countries.

D. Create a video to illustrate "all" the business opportunities.
    1. This will also serve as a strong communication by portraying the modern Kingdom and its people and will show the importance of the Arab World as Trading Partners.
        a. Export a wide variety of products to Saudi.
        b. Imports other than oil.
        c. Multi-national labor pool already in place in Saudi.
        d. Money supply.

OBJECTIVE IV

SET UP AND MAINTAIN A DAMAGE CONTROL TEAM FOR FAST ACTION.

A. To counter negative comments from the media.
   1. Correct erroneous statements with positive facts.

B. To correct image issues from major sources and major cities.
   1. Show positive images and feature crime free society in a modern setting featuring the Saudi family unit.

C. To use factual data to support our position.
   1. Continue positive imaging.

D. To select and pursue only those issues we can change.
   1. We cannot instantly change all opinions; only time and persistence in following our public relations plan will produce the total picture we strive to achieve.
   2. We will evaluate media as it becomes known and respond in a consistent manner. We will not react with haste. We will be pro-active rather than reactive.

GENERAL STRATEGIES

I Set up office in Washington D.C. to start this project. Washington is where the action is. It is divided into three parts:

1. Government.
2. Special Interest Groups.
3. Communication Media.
   a. Washington has news bureau for over 500 out of town newspapers.
   b. U.S. News and World Reports and the National Observer are published in Washington.
   c. More than 175 trade publications have an editorial staff in Washington.
   d. Four major TV networks have their best people in Washington with their corresponding network shows.

II. Create working relationships with some of the five hundred thirty people in Congress as well as their administrative assistants, aides and staff. It is not necessary to impact many people for all work is done by committee members and their staff. There are no secrets on how to do this. It is hard work and persistence pays off.

   In a typical day the public relations person will spend 60% to 70% of his time gathering information by making calls, having brief meetings with key personnel in their offices, going to social events and generally becoming known to a select group. The members of the media are an important part of this group.

III. The data gathered must be interpreted and analyzed daily and the ability to anticipate tomorrow's news is important. Then this information is separated into categories of importance and the appropriate action is taken by releasing the data reflecting our objectives through:

a. Press Releases
b. Newspaper articles and ads
c. Media Events
d. Scheduled meetings
e. Mailings
f. News letters
g. University Seminars
h. Magazines

We will get the facts out and understood, for images are changed based upon political and social implications, and their interplay with public opinion.

It must be emphasized that important as media relations are, we cannot rely completely on the major media organizations. The longtime and deep rooted bias that is found in the major news organizations will present an unnecessary obstacle to our efforts. Alternative and well- targeted paths to the influence centers of the U.S. population will be found.

Objective: Radio Talk Show Hosts
Saudi Arabia is more like U.S. than many other Gulf Regions Countries.

Objective: U.S. Conference of Bishops
Saudi Arabia morality is very similar to Christianity.

Objective: U.S. and State Chambers of Commerce Executives
Saudi Arabia business ethics are on the highest plain, not the "raid and rape" mentality of some other countries.

Objective: Educators and Social Studies Teachers
A good strategy is to authorize an author to produce a book (possibly a Historical Novel) that can be pointed out as an authentic source to substantiate our position.

PUBLIC RELATIONS AIDS

Other vehicles for our progress will utilize existing communications professionals and techniques. To do this, we will enlist the aids used by consultant/public relations people the world over. We will use a "total" program approach to make sure that all elements of the Public Relations program have been intelligently and thoroughly planned:

Situation Analysis. We will analyze the current and anticipated environment with present attitudes and the identification of the "target" public and the media needed to maximize our efforts. This will be a multiple market exposure with individualized messages for each of the "target" publics.

Identify Key Opportunities. This flows from the above Situation Analysis and creates a clear picture of the problems to overcome and/or the opportunities presented and how to best present our story.

Advertising Strategies. We will test our methods and results with a performance monitoring technique to make sure we are on track and are moving in the right direction in changing attitudes and images, as well as educating. The normal methods to measure our effectiveness are:

* Column Inch Report - Shows how many items are in the news that we generated.
* Clip Board - A filing system of releases by category.
* Opinion Polls - Sample questions and answer polls on a selective audience will show how much attitudes and opinions have changed.

Methods of getting publicity - We will establish good relations with key personnel in the media, government and the business community so we can be effective in utilizing the following:
* Mail - Send letters to the editors for printing.
* Press Conference - We will create a media event.

James L. Dickson Jr.

  * Develop Mailing List - We will mail to our target publics on a regular or special event basis using the following methods to develop the list we want, to the people we select:

1. General Business Community - National magazines, Chambers of Commerce, civic groups, political groups, special interest groups, etc.
2. Financial Community - national magazines, banks and their key employees.
3. General Public - a target audience with messages suited to their individual criteria e.g. community leaders, officials, key politicians, managers of local radio, TV and newspapers, leaders of social and fraternal clubs and civic organization leader.
4. Buy Specialized Lists - brokers have special lists by many categories and government agencies have lists.
5. Thomas Register of Manufactures - this is a list of all manufacturers with their products listed. Many are presently engaged in business in Saudi.

Establish Files For Release and Articles - create a log book to detail release and job envelopes for storing of all materials.

Gather Information For Releases and Articles

- Newspaper articles
- TV stories
- Interviewing the political leaders, religious leaders, businessmen and famous people (especially Arab/Americans)

Prepare News Release and Articles
- Write releases and Articles
- Quote "experts" and re-release their materials

Distribute News Releases and Articles
- Use direct mail lists
- Hire outside mailing houses that specialize in doing this. One firm has 70,000 plus editors, broadcasting, syndicated

columnist by name, daily newspapers, wire and TV
stations, etc.

- Build a relationship with specific media to release items as
  desired.
- Send featured stories to publications to help make the
  Saudi more visible. As feature stories are printed, we will
  use them in a reprint for a direct mailing list, and if good
  enough will create a slide for our audio/visual
  presentation. We will prepare an audio/visual presentation
  for each of our target publics. In this way we will generate
  awareness and interest in specific groups of people to
  Saudi and will target specific public relations to them in a
  variety of vehicles to both certainly improve the Saudi
  image in a positive and low-key conservative manner.

James L. Dickson Jr.

SUMMARY

Now more than anytime in our history, is the opportune moment for a well planned and faithfully executed public relations program. Conversely, to do nothing at this time could, depending upon the length and casualties suffered in Desert Storm operations, deepen negative perceptions that Americans will develop for Arabs in general. Add to this that the enemies of Arabs will be capitalizing on events by increasing their multi-million dollar public relations campaigns. Therefore, the most important project Saudi Arabia could start at this time is the education of Americans that the people of Saudi Arabia have many similarities to Americans in lifestyle, philosophy, technology, and goals. Secondarily, there are marked differences among the people, philosophies and governments of other countries in the Gulf Region.

A high profile, media blitz type program could well have disastrous negative impact and the results would be difficult to overcome. Therefore, our approach is a hands-on long-term gentle approach using positive imaging of real people to effect positive reaction with factual posturing.

We will define our target publics, position our strategy and use proper media and communications technologies to accomplish our objectives without the use of media hype and blitz that are used every day by conventional advertising/marketing/public relations firms. Rather, we will approach our objectives conservatively and create vehicles for the long haul and not the short ride media campaigns use to "sell" products, people and corporations.

Our philosophy will be, "this public relations effort will use every factual element to develop positive convictions in the major influence centers of the U.S." We will utilize placement of favorable news designed to affect desired results into local, regional, national and international media and every other communication path. By targeting our publics to people who influence other people as well as people who can or will share our philosophy, our focus will always be on our goals – Modern/Positive Image of Saudi/Arabs.

We will develop our programs in markets of:
- High population centers
- Top universities
- Markets with a large Saudi/Arab population

- Seats of government
- Key influentials of public thought
  1. Political
     a. National (Congress, Senate)
     b. Local (City, County)
  2. Educational
     a. Major Universities
     b. Private Schools
  3. Social
     a. Civic Organizations
     b. Religious
  4. Business
     a. Multi-national
     b. Prominent Industrialist
     c. Those now doing business in Saudi Arabia

We will develop both short term (12-18 months) and long- term (2-5 years) goals. In the beginning we will proceed slowly and build a strong team that will reflect the posture as outlined in our objectives.

Our job will be complete and we will reach our goals when we can educate the world to see the Saudi through my eyes.

CHAPTER FIVE

In late 1997 I called Senator D'Amato's Syracuse office. My attorney, who went to law school at Syracuse University with the Senator, was not able to set up a date and suggested I might have better luck in making an appointment because I was acquainted with his District Director, Gretchen Ralph. He was right, as usual, and one phone call resulted in one meeting. I met with Gretchen on January 28, 1998 and she promised to help, although she had very little faith because the Senator had constituents that he had tried to help but with no success. One businessman actually took his case to court, won the trial, and still didn't get paid. All these cases were businessmen to businessmen. Imagine the added difficulty when you're dealing with the King and one of his Ministers as I am. Most attorneys want to be paid for their services, so my case isn't of any interest to attorneys of quality. It was obvious that legal remedies would not work.

I thanked Gretchen for any help she could give and offered suggestions on how and who could verify my story. In the end I knew there was a routine to be followed and I should be thankful for any effort on the Senator's part. Maybe, if enough letters and memos are written by different members of Congress, the 'squeaky gate might get the grease'. I certainly wanted to explore all options and if effort alone would help, I was on my way. This project of being paid for the work I did was now starting to take on a life of it's own. Sure, the money is important, but it was not the only issue.

Gretchen didn't waste any time to help me. She wrote to the U.S. Ambassador in Riyadh, Saudi Arabia the same day of our meeting and sent me a letter to notify me of her effort. The Ambassador, Wyche Fowler Jr., replied on February 11, 1998 and suggested that I write to the new Minister of Information, His Excellency Abd Al-Salam Al-Farsi, and he would forward it to the Minister.

Due to the fact that the Ambassador was not acquainted with my project, he thought that Dr. Clive Mohammad was a resident of Sarasota, Florida, and not the Chief of Dental Services, King Fahd Armed Force Facility in Jeddah, Saudi Arabia, and that he also lived at the base. To correct the impression of my work, I wrote to the

Ambassador on March 9, 1998, and tried to impress upon him the importance the King and Minister had placed on the project.

March 09, 1998

Dear Ambassador Fowler:

Thank you for your letter of February 11, 1998, to Senator D'Amato concerning my work for the Kingdom of Saudi Arabia. Following your suggestion, I will write a cover letter for the New Minister of Information for you to forward.

Please allow me to correct the impressions you have of my work and of my contacts:

   a. Almost all my work was done between me and my contact in Saudi Arabia. There were constant phone calls, many faxes and communications on a daily basis.
   b. One of my contacts in the US was with Dr. Soraya H. Al-Mashat, who was an Advisor, Information Office, for His Excellency, the Minister of Information.

Prior to this, Dr. Al-Mashat was the Political Advisor for the Minister of Information with an office in Jeddah.

Furthermore, in order to fully understand the importance the Saudi's placed on this project, Dr. Al-Mashat volunteered to resign her position in the Washington Embassy and dedicate her expertise to insure the success of this most important project, and as such was in contact with both me and attorney Siracusa on a regular basis over many months.

   c. The Second Secretary, Abdulrahman A. Al-Shaia, called me via a request from Minister Al-Shair to continue my work here and to create a proposal for presentation to the Washington Embassy and Prince Bandar, who would then forward my work to King Fahd who initiated my being hired for this project.
   d. After the project was hand carried to King Fahd and the Minister of Information, I had daily, and sometimes several contacts daily, to explain, change, and update my

work. This was an every day activity and I spent all my time fulfilling these requests from both the Minister and King Fahd.

  e. Dr. Clive Mohammed was well known by King Fahd and the Royal Family. Not only was he their personal dentist, but he was also Chief, Dental Services, King Fahd Armed Forces Hospital in Jeddah. He was well known at your Embassy in Jeddah and also among the Sheiks and many professional people that he introduced me to when I was in Saudi Arabia prior to the Gulf conflict.

I believe that I should point out that it was King Fahd and Minister Al-Sha'ir that contacted me and asked for me to do this project. It was also the Second Secretary that contacted me for the Minister and who kept in contact with me to arrange my work to complete the proposal and deliver same to the Embassy in Washington.

My work was not as you stated, claimed, it was long hard work on a daily basis with definitive financial arrangements stated to both me and my attorney, whose office I moved into to complete this project.

I also wrote to the new Minister of Information and included all correspondence to bring him up to date. It was not surprising that my letter was not acknowledged nor was there ever any reply. The Saudis are above replying to any request that does not advance their own well being. This did not stop our efforts, and as such the Senator wrote again to the Ambassador and informed me of this in his letter of March 24, 1998.

On April 21, 1998, he received a reply from the Ambassador. Please take note of how expertly he dismisses any attempt to help by his statement, "We have gone as far as we legally can with this issue and, as I stated in my previous correspondence, it is advised that Mr. Dickson consult with legal council in Riyadh to determine what course of action he should take." With advice like this we could rid our ranks of anyone foolish enough to believe that a Saudi attorney could or would bring a case for an American to the courts in Saudi Arabia. The US State Department, DOS, warns all Americans against going to this country and advises that they cannot protect you. Of course my own experience in Jeddah, Saudi Arabia with the American

Embassy refusing me admittance was more than enough to deter me of expecting any help from US sources.

It is obvious that Ambassador Wyche Fowler, Jr. did not get actively involved in this matter. The typical 'we can't help' correspondence in hope the matter would go away was his first reply. The fact was that Dr. Clive Mohammad was well known in Saudi Arabia to a large number of people including King Fahd, several Ministers, Princes and Princesses', and many other well-known Saudis, and not unknown as the Ambassador suggested.

Although I tried to set the record straight with truth based on facts, it was not enough to overcome my lack of VIP status. There are many duties for an Ambassador, but getting involved with me was not on his short list, and if good public relations could possibly be strained by pursuing my problem it was only good judgment to put the more important good of the Embassy well ahead of an individual's problem. I've been at this so long I actually understand and agree that the good of the many outweighs helping one American receive monies for his work. Also, helping one low-level American citizen is never high on any list when it comes to the Department of State.

Allow me to point out that the Ambassador's second letter totally ignored my request for help, but instead pointed out that the US Government could not represent me in my claim, and that his office had gone as far as they legally could. I have often wondered what legal help they gave me to achieve such a final conclusion. The Senator's office could not enlighten me on any effort they did other than reply to their correspondences and support the folly of me seeking a Saudi attorney.

Evidently even answering the Senator's request was too much of an effort, as indicated in the fax from one office employee to another. When I received this fax I quickly called the Senator's office and spoke to Gretchen. After thanking her for trying to help I mentioned the fax and apologized for having called twice and taking up her time in two meetings. She claimed she had not seen the fax and that no one in the Senator's office would make any statement to indicate that I was not always welcome in his or her office, and the help they gave me was what they did for all the Senator's constituents. I thanked her again and told her I would never contact the Senator's office again and he should not count on my vote in the next election. I was insulted that the fax stated, "I hope this will satisfy your consultant (and he'll leave you alone)."

While the Senator's office was trying to help me I tried again to go straight to the source and write a letter on January 22, 1998 directly to His Excellency Ali Hasson Al-Shair. This was my fifth correspondence to him and as with the others, I received no reply. Silence is golden they say. If that statement is true then the Saudis I wrote to all have a lot of gold but they certainly haven't shared any of it with me.

January 22, 1998

Dear Excellency:

Please refer to my correspondence to you of:

July 30, 1991
January of 1992
June 17, 1992
August 14, 1995

There has been no acknowledgement that you have received the correspondence referred to above. I have asked United States Senator, Alfonse D'Amato, to channel this letter through his office in hope that there will be a response.

I am requesting to be fairly compensated for the work I did for the Kingdom of Saudi Arabia over a period of three years. This project was agreed upon with your intermediary, Dr. Clive Mohammed, who represented that your office had agreed upon paying for the project and all expenses connected therewith. Specific dollar amounts were discussed and agreed upon with me and Dr. Mohammed and are outline in the attached compensation page.

Dr. Clive Mohammed suggested I use attorney Joseph Siracusa for the project, and attorney Siracusa did accompany me on a trip to

Washington, D.C., New York City and at Dr. Mohammed's suggestion, with me to Dr. Mohammed's home in Sarasota, Florida. The express purpose of this trip was to talk to you by phone with Dr. Mohammed present. It was on this call that we brought you up to date on the progress that we achieved.

The four days in Florida were highlighted when you and I finally talked that Sunday. We agreed that the project was urgent and that I should get started right away. As a matter of fact, I am sure you will recall that you requested that I come to Saudi Arabia on Thursday to meet with you and King Fahd.

Unfortunately, it was at this time that the war in the Middle East was escalating and my trip was postponed. Your office decided that because this project was so important, that I should devote all my time and energy towards it, and to stop all other consulting I was doing and hoping to do.

I complained about my cash flow but was reassured my compensation, already agreed on, would catch up with me, and that I was on a five year contract with King Fahd with payments from your office.

For the next six months I worked full time on the Public Relations Project to improve the image of Saudi Arabia in the United States. During this time I made several trips to New York City and Washington, D.C., and had several conversations with Abdulrahman A. Al-Shaia, Second Secretary at the Royal Embassy of Saudi Arabia in Washington, D.C.

The first draft of the proposal was completed and the Second Secretary then requested that I present the proposal to the Royal Embassy, pursuant to your instructions. I traveled to Washington, D.C., and met with Dr. Soraya H. Al-Mashat and Dr. Mohammed. We spent one day going over the proposal and then I was instructed not to deliver the proposal to the Embassy, but rather have Dr. Mohammed personally take it back to Saudi Arabia and present it to you and King Fahd.

During the next seven months, weekly conversations and revisions were made, correspondence to complete the proposal were faxed and mailed, and finally the project was then approved. The next three months were spent on funding the project and I, once again, traveled to Washington, D.C. to take steps to implement the project. During this time, I was able to find office space, interviewed people to work

James L. Dickson Jr.

on the project, and had meetings with a public relations consultant and generally did whatever was required to begin to accomplish the objectives outlined in my proposal.

All during these twenty-five months, I devoted my full time to the project with the knowledge and confidence that you would honor our agreement.

Unfortunately, the project never started, and in retrospect it is easy to speculate that if it had been, the relationship between the United States and Saudi Arabia would most obviously be improved.

It might not be too late to start!

Sincerely,
James L. Dickson, Jr.

Compensation Page

I. Project Proposal	$500,000
II. Monthly Compensation @	$25,000
For 25 months	$625,000

Since I was constantly reassured that the agreed upon compensation would be forthcoming, I advanced and paid for the following:

- A. Outside Consultant Fee
- B. Phone Calls
- C. Fax Costs
- D. Air Fares
- E. Car Expenses
- F. Hotels
- G. Meals
- H. Parking, Tolls and Rented Cars
- I. Office costs
- J. Miscellaneous

III. In addition, and once again, with the assurance from Dr. Mohammed, I incurred attorney's fees in the amount of $130,290 to the suggested attorney which, to this date, remains unpaid.

In addition to this going on I was busy on the phone to anyone of influence who could carry my message to the US State Department, members of the Saudi Royal Family and to members of Congress. On May 13, 1998 I wrote a letter to His Royal Highness Prince Bandar and it was hand carried to his office along with other correspondences that would explain my dilemma. I was also talking to Jean Donalty of Congressman Sherwood Boehlert's Utica office, and had meetings with her to fully acquaint her with the details needed if we were to be successful in finding someone in authority that would take a personal interest and move the process to a higher level.

Congressman Boehlert's office went directly to the Department of State (DOS) in Washington and to the Saudi Embassy in Washington, as stated in their May 30, 1998 letter. The results were that David Sullivan, Attorney-Advisor for International Claims and Investment Disputes, DOS, was assigned to assist me. Mr. Sullivan gave freely of his time when I could reach him and it is my sincere belief that he tried, in every way he was permitted, to help me. As the story unfolds you will find out that within the Department of State (DOS), the levels of the people determine what they are permitted to do. Mr. Sullivan was able to write letters and make phone calls to and on a low level of authority. In a word, he was limited, limited, limited. His first letter was to Abdullah Al-Athel, Commercial Attache, Embassy of Saudi Arabia in Washington.

He talked to Al-Athel on June 30, 1998 and sent him a letter I had written to Prince Bandar with his cover letter dated July 2, 1998. When I received this correspondence I started calling Al-Athel and after many phone calls over a period of four months, I finally reached him. That was the good news. The bad news was that the Commercial Attache was the wrong person and did not, could not, handle any claims that had to do with the Royal Family. He told me he was not permitted to give me any information, including who was the right person at the Embassy for me to talk with, and if my project had been with a Saudi businessman, he would have settled this matter a long time ago. I was irritated that four months had been wasted by the DOS not knowing even who to contact. This lesson I learned over and over again. Simply stated, the Department of State was not well informed at my level of contact with anyone in authority from Saudi Arabia.

Ginny Pratt of the Saudi Desk worked with David Sullivan to advance my case. Ginny actually had met the Minister of Information Ali Al-Shair at an Embassy party in Saudi Arabia when she worked there. Again, her level of contact was similar to David Sullivan and at that level no decisions could be made. At that level they could not even write or phone any of the Saudis I had dealt with. The frustration grew and one day I got lucky and actually talked my way into a phone conversation with the gentlemen who dealt directly with the First Secretary, Saudi Embassy in Washington. Adel Al-Jubeir was Prince Bandar's assistant and could definitely move the process towards a decision. Again, I was not able to reach Adel Al Jubeir because he was at too high a level to waste his time with me. I called and called but could not get by his security.

David Sullivan and I talked frequently and Congressman Boehlert's office also contacted him, and on December 11, 1998 David Sullivan sent me a letter explaining he had contacted, by transmitted letter, John Moran, Economic Counselor, US Embassy, Riyadh and had sent him a cable stating:

"Enclosed as described in a forthcoming cable are two packets of materials concerning Mr. James Dickson. The first packet contains correspondence and information for forwarding to the Saudi Minister of Information. The second packet contains additional documents for your information only, which are not to be forwarded to the Saudi Government. Please contact me if you have any questions. Thank you for your assistance."

This cable was dated November 20, 1998 and became one of several very important documents to prove my case. Yes, it is necessary for me to prove to all who will take the time to become acquainted with the facts, that what I said I did was actually done and that the people I claim were involved were actually involved. If I never receive any compensation, and history strongly supports that I will not, then at least this economic disaster I put my family through will prove that my problem was that I trusted a King and Minister of the Kingdom of Saudi Arabia despite all warnings not to do so.

I never gave up calling First Secretary Adel Al-Jubeir and in late 1997 finally caught up to him when he was all alone working during a holiday. We had a very long conversation with him politely telling me he knew all about me and had received and read all of my correspondences, and that I was the victim of a sad plot that occurs from time to time when people in Saudi Arabia pose as members of the Royal Family and take advantage of Americans eager to do business in Saudi Arabia.

When I told him I had talked on the phone January 13, 1991 with the Minister, he said, "How do you know the person you talked to wasn't someone posing as the Minister?" Wow! Was this guy watching too many low budget TV movies or does Saudi Arabia really have problems like this? And I thought that Saudi Arabia was virtually crime free. He also told me that he was in charge of the Public Relations Project and had received proposals from over twenty people wanting to be a part of it, and he had never heard of me.

Our conversation concluded with the First Secretary requesting I write a letter to Minister Al-Shair refreshing his memory as to what I was to do for him and King Fahd and mail this letter to him. He would then send it by diplomatic courier directly to the Minister and assured me I would receive a reply. He was confident that the reply would not support my claims because he had sent the correspondence received at the Embassy to the Minister and he had "never heard of me" and had "no correspondence" from me.

I quickly called David Sullivan to inform him of my conversation with the First Secretary and the problem I had with his request. My problem was that I was being used to make the First Secretary aware of a project he and Prince Bandar knew nothing about. The fact that he was in charge in Washington of a Saudi Public Relations project that had been rejected by King Fahd and had never heard of me made it clear why I was never permitted to have a Saudi presence in the US. It then became clear that Phase I of my project was first to determine if such a project could succeed in America and if it could be managed and controlled in Saudi Arabia. No wonder there was secrecy from the start.

The big question to David Sullivan was, should I write that letter to Minister Al- Shair and explain what I was requested to do by King Fahd and Minister Al-Shair? Would this create problems internally and would I be in the middle? It was concluded that the fall out, if any, would not be serious and if I wanted to get paid for my services then this would be the best chance I might ever have.

I called the Saudi Desk and talked to Ginny Pratt and brought her up to date. She was excited and very interested in my conversation with the First Secretary. She suggested that if she could use my name, maybe she could get an appointment with him to go over my case. This sounded like a step in the right direction and it was agreed that Al-Jubeir could certainly be a strong advocate for my being paid. Ginny was successful in setting up a meeting and reported back to me on the outcome. The most notable part of our conversation was her bottom line comment, "I have good news and bad news. The good news is I met with the First Secretary and this will be very helpful for me in my career. The bad news is I couldn't do anything for you." Straight out what she meant was; I helped my career but I can't help you. I was happy for Ms. Pratt, congratulated her on her personal success, and started to write the correspondence that First Secretary Adel Al-Jubeir wanted.

CHAPTER SIX

The First Secretary's request to 'refresh' the memory of Minister Al-Shair by sending my correspondence directly to him at the Saudi Embassy was a problem for me; I searched my conscience and finally decided I had little choice if my mission to get paid was to have a chance to succeed. The first step was to change his opinion, if in fact what he stated was really his opinion that I was 'set up' by a group of 'con' people to create a Public Relations Project for the Kingdom of Saudi Arabia. The complete absurdity of this premise made me sure this was first a smoke screen. After all, Dr. Mohammed and I were involved in a commercial project in Saudi Arabia worth hundreds of millions of dollars, and Al-Jubeir was aware of this. I decided to stop this idea at once by giving him details he would check out in Saudi Arabia and in his own Embassy. My plan worked; for he was later to deny that he made any of these comments to me.

The letter I sent him on February 23, 1999 stated what he requested me to do, as well as made clear that I would not 'buy in' to his excuse. This letter and the letter to Minister Al-Shair will become more important as it will be additional documents to prove all that I stated as well as all that I claim. It becomes part of the proof that will be ignored by the Saudis, three Senators and all the people in the Department of State. Only Congressman Boehlert would allow me to present my facts and this made all the difference in his judgment to help me. It is not clear to me why no one else in my government wanted to know what happened. My guess is that it's a simple case, at least for the Department of State, that proof of what I did would negatively effect their relations with this oil-rich country, and when you compare the costs to America in dollars and American lives that have already been sacrificed, it is a no-brainer that I will not have a chance.

51

James L. Dickson Jr.

February 23, 1999

Dear Mr. Al-Jubeir:

In reference to your request that I write to his Excellency, Ali Al-Shair to confirm my employment to King Fahd and Minister Al-Shair, please find a journal of dates and facts that outline the major and pertinent events. This, I hope, will convince you of the legitimacy of my employment.

Your suggestion that I was "set up" by Dr. Clive Mohammed for his personal and private gain and that this was a fraud Dr. Mohammed "ran" on me is not possible when you carefully study the chronology of the facts and events.

For this to be true, his Excellency Ali Al-Shair, Second Secretary Abdulrahman A. Al-Shaia, Dr. Soraya Al-Mashat and life-long friend Irma Mohammed would all have had to be partners to conspire to deceive me.

Please note that this project started prior to the Gulf War and before you received twenty plus requests for a public relations project from such people as the Chancellor of Germany, America's presidents and vice presidents who contacted King Fahd, Prince Bandar and yourself.

Understand, I had no voice or control over the scope of the project and the rules of operation. Like any professional with any integrity, I followed the directions given to me and as all information was on a "need to know" basis, my activities were not a public matter.

At the time, I was not aware that this was a special project by King Fahd and Minister Al-Shair and that the Embassy was not in the loop. I requested many, many times that I work through the Embassy and report to Prince Bandar and/or a subordinate of his. I very much wanted a local US presence to coordinate and give final approval to any and all special news events that I planned. If you read my proposal, it would be clear how important this was to both myself and the success we all hoped to achieve.

Back to your premise that I was "used" and this was not a formal and legitimate project between me and the Kingdom of Saudi Arabia and that I never talked personally to Minister Al-Shair. Please allow me to show a "time line" of events that I believe proves all that I state and more"

1. First phone call came from King Fahd's office followed by a phone call from Minister Al-Shair's office; with the third call a private and personal call from Dr. Clive Mohammed from his private phone.
2. Phone call, October 19, 1990, that the Minister had approved the project and monies would follow.
3. November 27, 1990, phone call that requested I was to come to Saudi Arabia and have a formal meeting with King Fahd and Minister Al-Shair. I faxed my agreement to a private number for delivery to Dr. Mohammed. This fax created a problem.
4. December phone call from Dr. Mohammed for a meeting in Sarasota, Florida with my attorney as requested by Minister Al-Shair.
5. Phone call with Minister Al-Shair from Dr. Mohammed's in Sarasota, Florida on January 13, 1991 when he set up my trip to meet with him and King Fahd on January 17, 1991.
6. Twelve days later, on January 25, 1991, after my trip was delayed due to the escalation of the Gulf War, the Second Secretary, Abdulrahman A. Al-Shaia called me and stated, "His Excellency, Minister Ali Al-Shair had contacted the Embassy and he was directed to call me and coordinate my creating a formal proposal as soon as possible for delivery to King Fahd and Minister Al-Shair."
   a. Is it logical to assume that the Embassy and the Second Secretary were also involved in this giant scheme, and that my knowledge was needed for this group of dishonest people to make a profit? Certainly, they could have run the "scam" without me.
7. On February 5, 1991, we had a meeting in Washington with Dr. Mohammed and Dr. Soraya Al-Mashat, a trusted employee of Minister Al-Shair that was sent by him to work in the Washington Embassy and who reported to him on a regular basis.

8. February 6, 1991, meeting in Embassy with Second Secretary and permission was given to do a survey of the Embassy and include materials and information in my proposal.

Is it really possible that so many people, two of whom were trusted employees of the Kingdom of Saudi Arabia, all planned to take advantage of me and use me for two and a half years? Could I really have meetings in your Embassy, do a survey, and use documents in my proposal? Is this possible?

It is now clear to me why I was not permitted to deliver my proposal to the Embassy. This was a special project set up to be run through the Minister of Information office and approved by the King. The Embassy was not to be involved. All my activities were to be coordinated directly from the Minister of Information office. Dr. Soraya Al-Mashat would be my only local Saudi contact.

Thank you for your assistance. I wish this had been a more open project, but now I understand the secrecy. If you need more information, I am at your service.

Respectfully,
James L. Dickson, Jr.

Following is the letter that I wrote to Minister Al-Shair.

February 23, 1999

Your Excellency:

I need your help! I am enclosing facts and dates to refresh your memory as to what transpired relating to the public relations project that I was hired to do by you and King Fahd.

It all started with a phone call from Dr. Clive Mohammed, Chief of Dental Services, Armed Forces Hospital, Jeddah, who was the dentist to King Fahd, the Royal Family, other high officials and friends. Dr. Mohammed asked me if I could create a public relations project for the Kingdom of Saudi Arabia, a project that was very dear to King Fahd.

I politely declined and offered as reasons: the time it would consume, the enormous scope of such a project, and the many other reasons why this project would be difficult to do.

Clive called me from your office with more details. Although I was still not willing to commit, he suggested I think it over and would call me for my answer.

On Clive's third call, I accepted with strict conditions upon the terms. Two important considerations were: whom would I report to and the economics involved.

Clive reported back to me two days later that you would be in charge and all final decisions would flow from your office, which he would coordinate. He instructed me not to take any consulting projects as this was to take up all my time and I would be well compensated, and that you had agreed on $25,000 per month, the same amount he knew that I was paid by the Puerto Rican government for my consulting services a few years earlier.

My work was divided into three categories: I would do research, create a formal presentation, and on a continual basis keep Clive up-to-date on all news, etc., that pertained to the project. As you know, we exchanged news releases back and forth.

During July, August, September, and October, I daily worked the plan, and on October 19, 1990 received word that you approved the project but more data was needed for King Fahd.

On October 31, 1990, Clive called and stated that you needed an "outline of the proposal". This was created and sent.

On November 27, 1990, Clive called and I was requested to come to Saudi Arabia and meet King Fahd and you, and I was to fax him my reply. That fax got me into trouble, because it stated both King Fahd's name and your name and was read by someone before Clive received it.

Clive called in December and set up a meeting for my attorney and I to meet him at his house in Sarasota, Florida on January 11, 1991. We had meetings January 11, 12, 13, and 14 and on January 13, 1991, Clive finally reached you by phone at your residence. You stated many kind and complimentary words and said "Let's start it now, give DR. Clive your passport information to fly to Saudi Arabia on January 17, 1991 as the King wants to meet with you." I agreed, and Dr. Clive was going to escort me to the meeting. This trip was delayed because the Gulf War escalated.

Twelve days later on January 25, 1991, the Second Secretary, Abdulrahman A. Al-Shaia of the Royal Embassy of Saudi Arabia in Washington, D.C. called with greetings from you and that I was to finish the formal proposal as soon as possible and deliver it to the Embassy for him to forward directly to you.

The Second Secretary and I talked several times with him telling me about the urgency of the project. On January 28, 1991, he called and gave me a final date of February 6, 1991 to finish and deliver the proposal to him at the Embassy.

Clive called on January 29, 1991 and told me to stop all correspondence to the Embassy and he would meet with me on February 5, 1991 in Washington.

On January 31, 1991, I met with the advertising/public relations executives in my Syracuse office and again on February 1st and 2nd to go over and finalize the proposal.

On February 4, 1991, I had my proposal privately viewed by an executive of a large prestigious agency. It was graded outstanding and a $500,000 price tag was put on it.

On February 5, 1991, I met with Clive and Dr. Soraya Al-Mashat in her building, but at an apartment of a vice president of Mobil Oil where Clive was staying. We spent many hours going over the proposal and I was then instructed that I could NOT deliver the proposal to the Embassy and they gave me explicit reasons why I could not allow the Embassy to see the proposal. Dr. Clive decided that he would hand carry the proposal to you and King Fahd and my money would be sent at once. Reluctantly, I agreed.

Dr. Clive accompanied me to the Embassy on February 6, 1991, where we met Dr. Al-Mashat, had lunch at the Embassy prior to my 1 p.m. meeting with the Second Secretary.

After the meeting, I was given a tour of the Embassy and allowed to do a survey of the Embassy. In this survey, I discovered that the Embassy monitored all media and twice per day news releases were created for review by the Embassy.

This discovery was very important to me because it would save me at least three people for my project, and I would finally have a local authority to work with.

This idea was soundly rejected and I was told not to have any further contact with the Embassy.

February 9, 1991—Meeting with Clive in Washington.

March 5 and 9, 1991—Faxed material to Saudi Embassy, articles were on Palestine. These articles to be sent by Clive to your office.

March 11, 1991—King Fahd finally approved contract. Dr. Clive to go over all budget details with you, including monies owed:
    a. $500,000 for proposal
    b. $225,000 for nine months work

March 14, 1991—Clive will handle any and all problems. Embassy will not be involved. Meeting with you scheduled for March 19 on my monies and new budget for office in Washington, people, and my annual salary.

March 24, 1991—Phone call from Soraya on progress from Clive.

March 25, 1991—Phone call from Dr. Clive—everything all set, working out my personal budget. I will go to Washington on April 8th to confirm office and equipment costs, plus interview people to start work in late summer.

April 8, 1991—Trip to Washington on office and people.

April 9, 1991—Phone call from Soraya. Just returned from Ramadan vacation and wanted to be updated on the project.

April 16, 1991—Phone call to Clive. Please have money sent. The past year I have spent all my own money, taking it from my retirement account. This is not in keeping with our agreement. He agreed to expedite.

April 20-26, 1991—Phone conversations back and forth with Clive on three questions from King Fahd, who would not proceed until he is satisfied with answers.

May 13, 1991—Clive states you are out of the country. I need to have answer for King Fahd when you return.

May 26, 1991—Completed my answer for Clive to give to King Fahd.

King Fahd had three major questions:

I. How to insure that the project would not produce negative results similar to what happened in Kuwait:
    a. Don't use any advertising/public relations corporations.
        i.   Creative media blitz produces instant opinion with the fallout going in many directions and results cannot be predicted with accuracy
        ii. Cannot control material even with oversight;
        iii. Kuwait had to stop their method as it had produced very damaging public reaction. Public opinion started to become negative and not positive.
II. How to keep control:
    a. I suggested a close relationship with the Embassy with all new materials to be cleared through them. The Minister and Dr. Clive suggested I work closely with Dr. Clive and he would clear all new material with the Minister.
III. Size of Operation, Start and Future:
    a. Start in Washington and work slowly through major select cities.
        i. First office expansion in Syracuse.
        ii. Expand where large population of Arabs resided
            1. Maps and pages with population per each site.

June 10, 1991—Clive entertaining you and your staff. He will discuss my money and call me tomorrow.

June 11, 1991—Fax to Clive, where is my money and when do we start in Washington? Will not rent an office or hire people until all monies are received.

July 26, 1991—I sent a special delivery letter to Dr. Clive's office for delivery to you. Cannot fax due to security.

August 19, 1991 Clive stated you agreed with my letter and that King Fahd is delaying project due to the Embassy not being in the loop. It will take time to work this out; the project is still a definite go. I should keep Clive up-to-date with media facts and articles. I will continue to get paid. I kept asking when?

September, October, and November—Clive and I kept in touch and I continue to update him with phone calls, articles, and creating new ways to make the project more appealing.

November 17, 1991—Soraya sent back to Saudi Arabia. She is out of the project.

January and February, 1992—Clive insists project still alive and well, but internal problems more important and he will have a meeting with you on my money.

March 5, 1992—U.S. Congressman Jim Walsh sent a letter to you regarding my monies and me.

March 7, 1992—Clive is scheduled to have a meeting with you in ten days.

April 5, 1992—Clive states that you are in Mecca and a meeting is set for next week on my money.

For the next three months, we had little contact, and after August, 1992, all contact was about my money. Last contact on February 19, 1996, with Clive calling me to do a project for him, and he stated in his last contact with you in August, 1995, "You are going to start paying me at the rate of $100,000.00 per month until all monies are paid."

I still have not given up on being paid for the work I did, although I have never received a reply from you on the correspondence sent.

Is it possible you have not received any of my letters? If you have and answered, your correspondence has never reached me. If you have not replied to my letters, WHY?

Clive stated it would be insulting to you and King Fahd to have a formal, written contract. That sounded right. If I could not trust a King and a Minister of the Kingdom of Saudi Arabia to pay me for work they hired me to do, of what value would a written contract be for an American citizen living in the USA? Why would I agree to do a public relations project for them in my country? Obviously, this made sense to me, and still does.

Hoping this finds you in good health and that you will kindly reply and make arrangements to pay me a fair and equitable amount for the work I did.

Congratulations on your new appointment.

Sincerely,
James L. Dickson Jr.

While this was going on, Attorney-Advisor David Sullivan of the DOS was busy doing his best to help me. A diplomatic note was sent by the US Embassy on December 29, 1998 and received a reply via the Saudi Arabia diplomatic note dated March 1, 1999.

BEGIN TEXT:
WITH REFERENCE TO THE EMBASSY'S DIP NOTE NO. 1252 DATED 11/9/1419H. IN CONNECTION WITH COMPENSATION CLAIMS MADE BY MR. JAMES DICKSON, PRESIDENT OF DICKSON ASSOCIATES, FOR SERVICES HE ALLEGEDLY RENDERED TO THE MINISTRY OF INFORMATION, THE MINISTRY OF FOREIGN AFFAIRS WISHES TO ADVISE THE EMBASSY THAT THE MINISTRY OF INFORMATION HAS RECEIVED NO CORRESPONDENCES FROM THE ABOVE MENTIONED AND THAT THE ENTIRE CLAIM IS COMPLETELY GROUNDLESS AS FAR AS THE MINISTRY'S RECORDS ARE CONCERENED.
END TEXT.

Total denial! They have never heard of me, and even more to the point, they have 'received no correspondence' from me. What about the four (4) letters sent from my attorney's office directly to Minister Al-Shair? Probably were lost in the mail, or better yet, when the Minister left his job in August, 1995, all records were destroyed. OK, let's forget the first four (4) letters. How about the following:

- January 22, 1998—letter from J.L. Dickson to Minister Al-Shair
- March 9, 1998—letter from J.L. Dickson to Ambassador Fowler
- March 9, 1998—letter from J.L. Dickson to Minister Al-Salam

- May 13, 1998—letter from J.L. Dickson to Prince Bandar
- July 2, 1998—letter from Attorney-Advisor, DOS, David Sullivan to Al-Athel
- November 11, 1998—letter from Attorney-Advisor, DOS, David Sullivan to John Moran
- February 23, 1999—letter from J.L. Dickson to Al-Jubeir
- February 23, 1999—letter from J.L. Dickson to Al-Shair
- April 12, 2000—letter from Al-Jubeir to J.L. Dickson

How many times can they claim they never heard of me and have 'received no correspondences from me? How many times can they make statements like this and have the DOS agree with them and use this absurdity to deny me their help? Can it possibly be that the truth of an American must be sacrificed for the good of public relations with this important country that has so much oil? Is there a chance that not one of these correspondences ever reached the proper people? Of course not, as admitted in the First Secretary's April 12, 2000 letter to me and the correspondence of DOS, David Sullivan.

If we take the above list, read them carefully, then there is no chance that the Ministers of Information, Al-Shair and Al-Salam, and/or their people did not receive, read and not respond to the correspondence. Only one of these letters was written and sent by me. The other eight letters listed were in a variety of ways delivered to their destinations. The letter to Commercial Attache Al-Athel, addressed to Prince Bandar, was preceded by a phone call from DOS Sullivan to Prince Bandar. My letter to Prince Bandar was hand carried to his office and handed to his secretary. My letters to Al-Jubeir and Minister Al-Shair have been acknowledged as received by Al-Jubeir in his correspondence to me. The most telling of letters to understand what the Saudi game was and is will be the letter of April 12, 2000 from the First Secretary to me. It stated in the second paragraph:

"Several years ago when you first contacted the Embassy, you claim was forwarded to the appropriate authorities in the Kingdom. At the time, the Minister of Information indicated he knew of no agreement with you. I believe the American

Embassy in Riyadh received the same response when it requested information on your behalf. I explained this to you in our telephone conversation."

This statement is one hundred percent accurate. The Minister of Information responded to both the Saudi Embassy in Washington and to the U.S. Embassy in Riyadh that they never heard of me and never received any correspondence from me. Okay, let's start there. If they lost all the mail prior to 1998, but received the correspondence they replied to in 1998, how is it possible that they still had never heard of me or received any correspondence from me in 1999, as stated in their diplomatic note on March 1, 1999? Please remember, all nine (9) letters stated above were sent prior to March 1, 1999. How many times can you acknowledge receiving correspondence, make a statement you have no correspondence, and still be so arrogant and sure of yourself that you continue to abuse the writer? Not only do they not receive the correspondence they admit to receive but also phone conversations where they make statements and requests were never made. What a wonderful world to live in. Truth is without meaning unless articulated by only a few of the people in power. Of course, as we all have seen and read, even when those who have the power need to change their position, the written or spoken word was either taken out of context or was not understood. This got so bad in my case that the last time I would ever correspond to Ginny Pratt, DOS, Saudi Desk, was when she very carefully explained to me that I did not understand what the Saudis meant in their diplomatic note by saying 'received no correspondence'. So important is keeping good public relations with your Saudi contact that perception replaces fact, and spin replaces truth. If this is not enough to discourage anyone from pursuing their claim, wait until you read the letter from the DOS on all the help they gave me. Remember, this is my turn in the barrel. I only have two choices; quit and admit defeat, or keep trying and maybe I'll get lucky and find someone that will go against normal channels and actually be outraged enough to help me. This unfortunately never happened.

I decided to wear the First Secretary down by sending him one correspondence after another, each with the same purpose. First, to prove my case, and second to give him so many facts and so much data that he would be forced to change his views on the matter. I am sure they checked out all the data and knew what the truth actually is, but to admit and change their position has been a losing proposition. I was told by Dr. Clive that the money is not a problem, but the politics of admitting I was hired to do a project that never went forward will never happen. If you know the psyche of an Arab, you will understand the importance of not being wrong. There are reports of huge million dollar deals that were cancelled just to save face for the Saudi in charge, because he could not admit to making an error.

The first letter was sent to the First Secretary on April 21, 1999, and it gave him a 'time line of events' that he could verify. The data and specifics in this time line he could easily check, as there were phone calls from the Second Secretary of the Embassy, who reported to him. A mere check of phone bills for January and February 1991 would reveal that the Second Secretary did make the calls to rush my finishing the proposal for the King, and to invite me to bring the proposal to the Embassy on February 6, 1991. A check of the Embassy's records on February 6, 1999 would verify that I was admitted to the Embassy, and a check with Dr. Soraya Al-Mashat would verify that I had lunch there and went to my 1 p.m. meeting with the Second Secretary where the proposal for King Fahd and Minister Al-Shair was the sole purpose for the meeting. There were many other facts he could and probably did verify.

April 21, 1999

Dear Mr. Al-Jubeir:

The enclosed 'time line of events' will hopefully help you arrive at my position of the authenticity of my

63

employment by the Minister of Information, His Excellency Ali Al-Shair. Combine this with the more detailed correspondence sent to you on February 23, 1999 and you have factual account that proves all that I claim.

Certainly my information can be positively verified. Phone records from Saudi Arabia to me will verify dates, time and frequency. Phone records for the call from Sarasota, Florida to Minister Al-Shair can be checked for accuracy, and the several phone calls from your Second Secretary, Abdulrahman A. Al-Shaia, will verify his calls to me. To all this add the many phone calls from Dr. Soraya Al-Mashat to both me and my attorney and you will have a complete record of proof that all these people were involved in my employment for the Kingdom of Saudi Arabia, through the Ministry of Information office.

So many calls over so many months during 1990, 1991, and 1992 with high profile VIP employees of your government should serve as proof of all that I state, and the only question left is what happens next.

I have written many times and phoned many times and have not received even one phone call or one acknowledgement. It's difficult for me to understand what I have done not to be treated with normal courtesy and respect, especially in light of all my effort, time, and monies spent on behalf of the Kingdom of Saudi Arabia.

Please acknowledge that this correspondence has reached you. Let's resolve the problem to our mutual satisfaction.

Thank you!

Sincerely,
James L. Dickson, Jr.

The request for me to do a Public Relations Project

    I.   Phone call from Dr. Clive Mohammed from King Fahd's office requesting for me to create a public relations project for the Kingdom of Saudi Arabia in the United States.

    II.   Phone call from Dr. Clive Mohammed from Minister Al-Shair's office providing more details on the importance and scope of the public relations project.

    III.   Phone call from Dr. Clive Mohammed asking for my total commitment to the project. I agreed after the approval of two strict conditions I had insisted on was approved by Minister Al-Shair.

        1. Who would I report to?

           a. Minister Al-Shair

        2. Economics

           a. Monies guaranteed by King Fahd through the Ministry of Information office

    IV. Phone calls, correspondence, articles, etc. on a daily basis pertaining to the project.

Approval of the project I proposed

    I.   On October 19, 1990 Dr. Clive Mohammed called and stated, "Minister Al-Shair had approved the project I had proposed. Needed a proposal for King Fahd's acceptance."

    II.   On October 31, 1990 Dr. Clive Mohammed called and I was instructed to send an 'outline of the proposal' for delivery to King Fahd.

    III.   On November 27, 1990 a request for me to come to Saudi Arabia to formally meet with King Fahd and Minister Al-Shair.

        1. I faxed my approval.

    IV. December, 1990—Dr. Clive Mohammed called and set up a meeting with me and my attorney at his wife's house in Sarasota, Florida

        1. The meetings were held January 11, 12, 13 and 14.

           a. On January 13, 1991 Dr. Mohammed reached Minister Al-Shair by phone and after a lengthy conversation between me and Minister Al-Shair, I was instructed to fly to Saudi Arabia on January 17, 1991 to meet with both King Fahd and Minister Al-Shair. This flight was cancelled due to the escalation of the Gulf War.

Report from the Royal Embassy of Saudi Arabia in Washington, D.C.

I.   On January 25, 1991 Abdulrahman A. Al-Shaia, Second Secretary, Royal Embassy of Saudi Arabia in Washington, D.C. called with instructions from Minister Al-Shair for me to finish my formal proposal ASAP for immediate delivery to him so he could forward the proposal to Minister Al-Shair.

II. On January 28, 1991 Second Secretary Al-Shaia called to inform me he needed my proposal delivered to the Embassy on February 6, 1991.

III. February 5, 1991 I had a meeting with Dr. Mohammed and Dr. Soraya Al-Mashat, who worked for Minister Al-Shair stationed in the Washington Embassy, for an intensive and complete review of my proposal.

   1. I was instructed NOT to deliver the proposal to the Embassy and that Dr. Mohammed was to hand carry the proposal for presentation to King Fahd and Minister Al-Shair. The Embassy was not to be permitted to review the proposal.

IV. February 6, 1991—meeting with Second Secretary Al-Shaia in his office in the Embassy. Also attending the meeting were Dr. Mohammed and Dr. Al-Mashat.

   1. Had lunch in the Embassy

   2. Permitted a survey of the Embassy to see if they could be helpful in the project.

King Fahd gives approval

I.   On March 11, 1991 Dr. Mohammed called with the approval of King Fahd.

II. March 14, 1991 Dr. Mohammed called to inform me he was to be involved in the project in the daily matters and

that the Embassy would not have any part in the project, and that the monies owed to me would be paid soon.
1. $500,000.00 for proposal
2. $225,000.00 for the first nine months work
III. On March 25, 1991 I was instructed to go to Washington, D.C. on April 8, 1991 to confirm office and equipment costs, plus interview people to start work in late summer.
IV. April 8, 1991 I traveled to Washington, D.C. for data on costs and availability of people and office.

King Fahd's Three Questions
I. April 20-26, 1991—Phone conversations between Dr. Mohammed and myself on three questions King Fahd needed to begin formal operations of the project.
1. How to insure that the project would not produce negative results similar to what happened to Kuwait.
2. How to keep control.
3. Size of operation—Start and Future
II. On May 26, 1991 I sent my answers for King Fahd directly to Dr. Mohammed.

Money and Start Time to officially open office
I. June 11, 1991 sent fax on request to be paid and when do we officially start to rent office and hire people.
II. July 26, 1991 sent Special Delivery letter to Minister Al-Shair on monies and advantages to start project at once.
III. August 19, 1991 phone call from Dr. Mohammed that Minister Al-Shair agreed with my letter of July 26, 1991 but King Fahd was delaying project because of the problems created by the Embassy not being in the loop. It will take time to work this out.
1. Keep everyone up to date with articles and media facts so when we start we're up to date.

Five days later another letter. This was to go over the diplomatic note with a reference to a few times they replied, no correspondence. One sentence stated:
"It is not surprising that the Minister of Information office cannot locate all the work I did for that office in 1990, 1991, and 1992 when

correspondence sent by me in January, 1998, the U.S. State Department correspondence sent in the spring of 1998, and the correspondence sent by you from the Washington Embassy in the summer of 1998 is also lost."

I also asked him to check with Dr. Soraya Al-Mashat, a trusted employee for many years who worked for Minister Al-Shair and who was in constant contact with him.

She could verify the validity of my project. She alone could put to rest any question about who hired me and why she wanted to work for me on the project.

Four days later, another letter. This one could stop all speculation about what I was doing and for whom. In it I enclosed a personal hand written letter to me from Dr. Soraya Al-Mashat with her Vita (resume) enclosed. Dr. Al-Mashat wanted to assist me in my five year Public Relations Project and be my Saudi presence in the U.S. When reading her Vita please make a big deal out of the fact that Soraya was a Saudi woman who worked for her country in various capacities of authority, when Saudi women were not permitted a job under severe penalties. She was not only more than a decade ahead of her time, but was also a well paid officer and Director making decisions that only highly trained and trusted Saudis were privileged to do. Take note of her duties and in some cases use a little imagination of what she really was doing and you will understand her comment that, "Confidential nature of job prevents further detail." Also, the note of her education, publications, awards, traveling experiences and personal data all told she was one of a kind. A VIP in every sense of the phrase. Like Dr. Clive Mohammed, she was much more than she appeared and much, much more than her job title implied. No wonder they were so well acquainted.

Following is my letter to Al-Jubeir with Dr. Soraya Al-Mashat's letter included.

April 30, 1999

Dear Mr. Al-Jubeir:

Going through my files on the Kingdom of Saudi Arabia I found the enclosed correspondence from Dr. Soraya Al-Mashat. What makes this unusual is that there is a handwritten personal letter with signature as well as the normal typed correspondence.

Just more proof of all that I have stated. Proof that cannot be refuted. Proof that I could not create. Proof that came from a long-time trusted employee of Minister Al-Shair who knew about my project and wanted to be a part of it. An employee at the Embassy that most certainly was in the loop.

Hoping to hear from you soon so we can resolve this situation to our mutual satisfaction.
Thank you!

Sincerely,
James L. Dickson, Jr.

This is Dr. Soraya Al-Mashat's letter to me:

Dear Mr. Dickson,

Hope this finds you and yours in good health and spirit. As per our telephone conversation, enclosed is a copy of my vita. As mentioned to you my present capacity is not included. I will very much appreciate your opinion and suggestions.

Please give my regards to your family and Mrs. Dickson. If you have a chance to speak to Dr. Clive Mohammed say hello for me.

Thank you for your time and I will be talking to you soon. With best wishes.

Regards,
Soraya Mashat

VITA

Soraya Mashat

PROFESSIONAL GOAL:
A Management or administrative position in an International or Multi-National Organization for public relations, communications, research, external affairs, and/or media department. Relocation or travel are no obstacles

JOB HISTORY:

1986-Present

Ministry of Information, Information & External Affairs Department, Jeddah, Saudi Arabia
Position: Political Advisor
Duties: Planning, research, analysis and public relations.
(Confidential nature of job prevents further detail).

And

Ministry of Information, English services or Radio Jeddah, Saudi Arabia
Position: Director
Duties: Selection of programs; supervising productions; technical, content and script editing; research; planning and formatting the biannual layouts.

Present additional activities:

Saudi Gazette: A national Daily English Newspaper, Jeddah, Saudi
Arabia
Position: Reporter
Duties: Free lance reporter, writer, and editor.

Radio Jeddah: English Services, Second Channel, Jeddah, Saudi
Arabia
Position: Producer/Announcer
Duties: Producing, announcing, and editing programs both in English
and Persian, (Farsi).

Saudi Arabian Television: English Services, Channel II, Jeddah,
Saudi Arabia
Position: Editor/Announcer
Duties: Editing, Announcing television programs
1985
International Monetary Fund, External Affairs Dept. – Washington,
D.C.
Position: Assistant Editor
Duties: Conducted a content analysis of Finance & Development, a
quarterly publications of IMF, for four year period. (Independent
Contractor)

1983-1985

Royal Embassy of Saudi Arabia, Information Office- Washington,
D.C.
Position: Information Officer
Duties: Information coordinator for public, business and media
organizations; analyzing proposals, documents and media contents;
research & formatting for Saudi Arabia, an Embassy monthly
publication.
Reason for leaving: Transferred to Saudi Arabia, Ministry of
Information.

1982

World's Fair, Saudi Arabian Pavilion, Knoxville, TN
Position: Public Relations Officer
Duties: Providing information about Saudi Arabia to public and media organizations; press releases, and hosting international V.I.P.'s visiting the pavilion. (Independent Contractor)

1981

Saudi Arabian Educational Mission, Ottawa, Canada
Position: Academic Advisor
Duties: Communications with various universities throughout Canada to orient and assist Saudi students with their selected majors and course work. (Summer job)

1975-1977

Cement Company, Tehran Iran
Position: Corporate Analyst
Duties: Coordinating communication between the different departments; providing reports for implementing the company's policies and progress.
Reason for leaving: Continue graduate studies in the United States

1972-1977
Parss Toshiba Company, Tehran Iran
Position: Product marketing research, the design and implementation of advertising campaigns.
Reason for leaving: Training at the University of Geneva, Switzerland.

1970-1972

Peerless Company, Tehran Iran
Position: Executive Assistant
Duties: Supervision of office staff, responsible for the legal preparations required by the marketing department.

EDUCATION:

Doctorate of International Communications- Pennsylvania State University, 1985
Masters of Arts- Pennsylvania State University, Journalism/Advertising, 1981
Bachelor of Arts- University of Tehran Iran; English Literature/Marketing, 1973

PUBLICATIONS:

Saudi Women as Portrayed by American T.V., 1985. Pennsylvania State University
Articles of political nature in <u>Saudi Gazette</u>, Saudi Arabia's national daily English newspaper, since 1986.

AWARDS:

Academic fellowship Grant Pennsylvania State University and scholarship from Saudi Arabian Government.

TRAVELING EXPERIENCE:

Traveled extensively throughout the Middle East, Asia, Europe, North America and Canada

PERSONAL DATA:

Marital Status: Single
Nationality: Saudi Arabian
Language: English, Persian (Farsi), and Basic Arabic

To quote from the First Secretary's letter of April 12, 2000 again:

"I also stated that conversations between you and Embassy employees with no authority to commit the Saudi Government, and who have long since left the Embassy, would not suffice."

The First Secretary was referring to Dr. Soraya Al-Mashat and Second Secretary Abdulrahman Al-Shaia. Imagine, Dr. Al-Mashat was sent to work in the Washington Saudi Embassy by Minister of Information Al-Shair after being the political advisor of the Ministry of Information office in Jedddah, Saudi Arabia. She was the only employee of Al-Shair in the Saudi Washington Embassy. Let's forget about her authority and ask a different question. If she worked for Minister Al-Shair and was in contact with him, knew all about my Public Relations Project and wanted to be involved in it, would she not be the perfect person for the Saudis to talk to about me? Is it slightly logical to even pretend I was not what I claimed and the project I did was for the King and the Minister as she, the Second Secretary and Dr. Mohammed all stated.

The Second Secretary was also a person of authority. In our meeting he told several stories of American VIP's soliciting him to do projects for the Kingdom of Saudi Arabia. This was part of his job description and he had the authority to be given my name, address and phone number so he could have me hurry up and finish the King's proposal, as requested by Minister of Information Ali Al-Shair. He certainly didn't get my name and phone number out of the local phone book to call me and tell me that King Fahd was in a rush for my proposal. If he did this without authority, I would be surprised if he is among the employed of Saudi Arabia. The bottom line of Al-Jubeir's letter was, please go away, stop bothering because we are not interested in paying you, so go bother someone else.

CHAPTER SEVEN

While I was trying to go straight to the source via the Saudi Washington Embassy, I was also busy soliciting help from the DOS and members of Congress. I made phone calls, sent information and had meetings whenever I could find a member of my government who would give me the time. The most effective member of Congress was Sherwood Boehlert, a Republican Congressman of many years. His District Director, Jean Donalty, did all she could do in her capacity to help and never refused to read and act on any information I gave to her. She made phone calls to the Department of State and forwarded the appropriate information. The problem was not one of her effort. The problem was that the level of contact was not on a high enough level to do more than have them write letters and send information. What a wonderful way to waste time. Members of Congress writing to members of the State Department and the State Department could not even act on a high enough level to illicit a response. This went on much too long and finally the Congressman wrote to me on May 20, 1999 that they had forwarded to both Sullivan and Ms. Pratt my last information. He sent regrets that all his efforts have been unsuccessful and expressed his dissatisfaction to both parties at the DOS. They had not been able to put enough pressure in their failed attempts to assist in processing my claim. Still trying to help he stated, "If you have any additional information or further questions or concerns, do not hesitate to contact me."

If my Congressman did not have enough clout maybe a Democrat Senator could move the ball down the field. New York State had just replaced Republican Senator Al D'Amato with Democratic Congressman Chuck Schumer. He moved into his Syracuse office and a local judge suggested I call them.

I phoned Senator Schumer's Syracuse office on June 3, 1999, talked to Jill Harvey and set up an appointment for June 8. Her schedule became very busy that day so we changed the date to June 10. She promised to give me one hour to present my case, but again she had a big workload so we met for a little over thirty minutes, just enough time to rush through the material I wanted to present. To make up for the lack of time, she asked an assistant, Steve Coste, to make copies of the material and she would go through it and get back to me. Before I left she asked, "What can Chuck Schumer do for Jim Dickson?" I told her I would call her back with the exact specifics I thought would help to solve my problem. She then asked, "Why didn't you give the Senator the fax from Senator D'Amato before the election, as it would have helped us in the election." Of course that is why I didn't give anyone that fax. I didn't wish to be involved in an election where I didn't know one of the candidates.

Five days later, on June 15, I called but she was out of the office. I called the next day and she was in meetings all day. On June 17, an aid to Senator Schumer, Eric Schultz, took my call and stated that she was too busy to take my call. He would give her the message and she would get back to me. Of course this never happened. Being persistent, I made the following calls without talking to her or her returning any calls:

- July 6 at 1:30—in meeting
- July 6 at 3:07—on phone, she wants to talk to me and will call back
- July 12 at 10:45—not in
- July 13 at 3:20—on the phone, left message
- July 27 at 9:55—no one at office, left message on answering machine
- July 27 at 2:30—on phone of course and always a conference call
- January 25 at 11:30—no one there but the answering machine

By now the message was loud and clear. Jim Dickson was not important enough for anyone in Senator Schumer's Syracuse office to waste his or her time on. Was the fact that I was a registered Republican the reason for such sloppy treatment? Or was it that I never contributed to the Democratic Party. I never found out but 'chalked' it up to normal procedure at most Congressional offices when dealing with the public.

Maybe it was just the Syracuse office. I called the Senator's Washington office on September 21, 1999 and talked to staff assistant Dan Wilson. After a few minutes I realized that Dan Wilson had no idea what my call was about. He explained that he was hired only six weeks ago, and he would ask for advice and he or someone else would call me back. In the meantime I should call Mike Cusick in the New York City office and maybe he could help. When I called Dan Wilson back he informed me that the Washington office does not do 'case' work and Mike Cusick in the New York office was really the correct person to handle my case. After five more calls to Cusik, where no one answered the phone or I was put through to Cusick's voice mail, I finally gave up.

When I told a local judge about my failure to reach anyone by phone in New York City he offered the comment that the Senator was having problems with his New York office. If my experience was typical, the Senator was having more than problems in New York. His transition from Congressman to Senator was not as smooth as he might have desired, and his constituents were not being served very well. So much for the spin that members of Congress work for the people.

Having no success with two Senators I decided to go to a person who never held an elected political office that I was aware of, but who was thinking of moving to New York State and running for Senator. Hillary Clinton was really a great choice to help me. After all, she was the President's wife and had been involved in politics for most, if not all of her adult life. A phone call from her could easily bring a solution to my problem.

On July 31, 1999 I wrote Hillary Clinton asking for her help. I was remiss and did not check the spelling of her first name and sent the letter with only one "L" in Hillary. I hoped she would forgive this oversight on my part and it would not stop her from helping me.

July 31, 1999

Dear Hilary:

I need your help! If you were presently a New York Senator I would be the first person at your congressional office explaining to one of your staff, in great detail, the very serious problem I have had as a

77

consultant for two and one half years for King Fahd and Minister Ali Al-Shair of the Kingdom of Saudi Arabia. (Minister Al-Shair left office August 1995.)

One well-placed phone call by you would get the results that over two years of efforts by past and present members of Congress and the State Department could not and have not been able to do. Unfortunately, their level of contact is not on a high enough level to even obtain a response to my correspondence. The Saudis simply do not reply because they know our system at that level does not require any action to be taken.

Their reply to a diplomatic note sent by the State Department was they had received NO correspondences related to J.L. Dickson. This was after the State Department had sent documents from me on three occasions and I had sent the documents on six occasions. Again they understand that by ignoring or denying my claim the problem to them would go away. That the American political system isn't set up to do more for the average American citizen than a letter or phone call, and the courtesy of a reply is not necessary if you want the problem to go away.

Yes, I fully understand that for me to ask for an hour of the First Lady's time is not normally done. But this letter appeals to that special person running to become a Senator of New York, and she has abilities that other members of Congress do not have. The ability to actually solve problems and not just talk about solutions.

One hour of your time and one phone call would make a huge difference in the lives of the entire Dickson family. It would correct a wrong and send a message that each and every American is important, not just our VIP's. Isn't it time that the average American receives the help from government that is now reserved for the few?

Will you help?

Sincerely,
James L. Dickson, Jr.

Hillary never answered, but Congressman Boehlert was busy on my case. He again contacted Ginny Pratt and David Sullivan at the Department of State. They, of course, assured him they were working hard to get him some kind of response and are very much aware that he is trying to see that my case receives top priority. Again, in his August 6, 1999 letter to me he requested I contact him if I had any more questions or ideas I wanted to share with him.

I was becoming embarrassed that this member of Congress cared so much, tried so hard to help, but the Department of State was unable even to make contact with this most popular oil-rich country. I kept thinking how America rushed to that country's side in 1990 and 1991, with American men and women fighting and dying to protect them, and they did not have the courtesy or decency to even reply to an American member of Congress. Do we need their oil so bad that we forgive any and all their actions, or is oil lobbying so powerful that the Saudis know who they must play ball with. I put my money on the lobbyist.

The Saudis did not reply but the Congressman's letter to me on September 16, 1999 had an enclosure from Barbara Larkin, Assistant Secretary, Legislative Affairs, Department of State. The Congressman also spoke again to David Sullivan and received his assurance that the DOS will monitor their inquiries to the Saudis until they receive a reply. How about that? Is it really possible that I am going to be helped by the U.S. State Department? I was hopeful but not optimistic.

Barbara Larkin's letter to the Congressman dated August 31, 1999 promised that they shared my frustration with the total lack of response from the Saudi government and both the Department and our Embassy in Riyadh will assist me. They even went so far as to contact the First Secretary and request that he reply to my inquiries at his 'earliest convenience'. Wow! What pressure. Just imagine, they request he responds at his earliest convenience. Another bottom line. They failed, and there was no response to the Department of States's request. So much for what they call going the extra mile and doing all in their power to help me. With help like this no wonder so little gets done in Washington.

I got tired of waiting and decided I would put my kind of pressure on Al-Jubeir. I wrote him the following letter and in strong but polite factual statements told him what I thought of the Kingdom of Saudi Arabia totally ignoring my letters, and more importantly completely ignoring letters from the State Department and a member of Congress from a country that still is protecting them from all enemies with a military presence in their country. To make sure I would finally receive a reply, I copied my letter to the following:

- Crown Prince Abdullah
- Prince Bandar
- Secretary of State Albright
- Congressman Sherwood Boehlert

December 7, 1999

Dear Mr. Al-Jubeir,

It has been almost a year since you promised me that if I wrote a letter to His Excellency Ali Al-Shair and sent it to you at the embassy, you would forward this document in a diplomatic pouch directly to him. You assured me that I would most definitely receive a reply. You also guaranteed me that if Minister Ali Al-Shair confirmed that he and I talked and that he invited me to Saudi Arabia because King Fahd wanted to meet me in person, the money promised for my thirty plus months of work would be paid at once, because the Kingdom of Saudi Arabia honors all her commitments and obligations.

Not only did I comply with your requests, but I sent five (5) additional correspondences directly to you, the last one in April, 1999. In these documents I presented a time line of events with dates and names plus phone calls made and received, all of which can be verified. Also, very verifiable are phone calls from the Second Secretary, Abdulrahman A. Al-Shaia, where he represented that Minister Al-Shair requested he contact me and have me finish my proposal, requested by King Fahd, by February 6, 1991 and deliver it to the embassy. This was done and the proposal was hand carried to King Fahd and Minister Al-Shair by Dr. Clive Mohammed who remained in constant contact with me.

In addition the U.S. State Department also sent you many correspondences from three departments requesting you to contact me. To this date I have not been contacted by you by phone or letter. Total silence has been your answer to my requests and to the requests of the U.S. State Department.

Certainly you can understand my disappointment and frustration that not only am I being treated very poorly, but the U.S. State Department and all my congressman's efforts as well are being totally one hundred percent ignored. This lack of cooperation between Saudi Arabia and the U.S. State Department speaks volumes for the relationship between our two countries and how you feel about Americans. Frankly, I'm surprised since American men and women rushed to your aid in the gulf conflict and America is still keeping a military presence there to protect your country from any and all conflicts.

Yes, you do understand how the American political system works, from the efforts of members of congress to the degree of help or lack of help the State Department gives to an average American Citizen. But this may all change soon as America has several presidential candidates that promise no more considerations and privileges for the rich and famous, and that each American will have a 'seat at the table' and government agencies will serve us all equally.

81

James L. Dickson Jr.

Hopefully I won't have to wait until our elections are over for you to contact me. So as the new millennium races towards us, lets start the New Year off on a positive note by talking, meeting and bringing this ten-year project to an end. You will find me ready, willing, and able to meet you more than half way. Will you be willing to reach out and go the rest of the way?

Sincerely,
J.L. Dickson Jr.

It took a long time, and additional letters from the Congressman but on April 12, 2000 the First Secretary wrote to me at the request of Prince Bandar. Prince Bandar also replied to the Congressman the next day. Finally, a small victory. Not one you can be proud of, but at least a move in the right direction. As in all negotiations you don't make progress until there is dialogue, and this might be the start to bring this project to a welcome conclusion.

82

CHAPTER EIGHT

Congressman Boehlert did not give up. His letter of January 7, 2000 to me explained his new strategy. He would by-pass the State Department people that were unable to even elicit a reply of any kind, and write a letter directly to Prince Bandar and to DOS Secretary of State Madeleine Albright. In his second letter to Prince Bandar, dated January 7, 2000, he pointed out his previous letter to the Ambassador was never acknowledged and that to that date all inquiries have gone unanswered.

He followed his letter to Prince Bandar with a strong letter to Secretary of State Albright.

February 24, 2000

Dear Madame Secretary:

I am enclosing a copy of a letter addressed to Adel al-Jubeir, First Secretary, Embassy of Saudi Arabia, by my constituent, James L. Dickson, Jr., J.L. Dickson Associates, regarding his efforts to file a claim for compensation with the Saudi Arabian government. On January 7, 2000, I forwarded Mr. Dickson's letter to Prince Bandar Bin Sultan along with a personal request that he be afforded the opportunity to present his case for consideration and appropriate compensation. To date, there has been no response from the embassy.

Since May, 1998, I have attempted to assist Mr. Dickson in his efforts to contact the Saudi government. I previously wrote directly to the embassy and have been in contact with the Department of State's (DoS) Office of the Legal Advisor and Saudi Arabian desk officer. While your staff has been responsive and has followed through on Mr. Dickson's behalf, no progress has been made to date in eliciting any type of direction from Saudi officials on how to proceed. It appears that written inquiries to the embassy are easily ignored.

Mr. Dickson is understandably frustrated and angry that his government and elected officials are unable to establish contact for him with the embassy. He has asked that I bring this matter to your attention. Mr. Dickson points out that on August 31, 1999, I received a letter from the DoS's Office of Legislative Affairs that stated "department officials will monitor this matter until Mr. Dickson has received a reply." I have enclosed a copy of this correspondence. Mr. Dickson points out that since this letter, DoS staff have had one meeting, written one other letter which was ignored, and have failed to call him to keep him updated on his case. What further steps can be taken at this point to assist Mr. Dickson?

I am enclosing background information which Mr. Dickson has provided outlining his situation and he is available to respond to any questions you may have regarding the work he did, contacts, etc.

Thank you for your attention and cooperation. I look forward to hearing from you.

With warmest regards,
Sherwood Boehlert

Again in March 22, 2000 the Congressman wrote to Secretary Albright and requested a reply. Guess she was too busy for no reply ever came. Still trying, he wrote again to H.R.H. Prince Bandar and requested a reply. I learned that the Department of State under Secretary Albright either did not have the means to establish a dialogue with the Kingdom of Saudi Arabia or didn't take the time to perform this normal perfunctory task. Let's recall that the Congressman's letter of February 24, 2000 to Secretary Albright pointed out explicitly that the DOS stated they will follow this matter until I received a reply, and since that statement was made, they had one meeting and wrote one letter, all of which were ignored by the Saudis. With public relations from our country to theirs like this, no wonder most of Europe and the entire Gulf region pays little attention to us except when we send money, food, and military equipment and supplies. How long before someone will get bold enough to tell us we're not needed and our advice is not sought unless preceded by promises and gifts. The number one military power in the world and we cannot even get a reply from a country we went to war to protect. Sad but true!

Still trying, Congressman Boehlert wrote another letter to the Ambassador, H.R.H. Prince Bandar on April 3, 2000, and on April 12, 2000 the First Secretary Al-Jubeir, instructed by his boss Prince Bandar, wrote his first letter directly to me. It took over two years for the Kingdom of Saudi Arabia to reply to this American's request. All the efforts of the U.S. State Department and members of Congress had little if any effect to bring about a response. It is my opinion that between Congressman Boehlert's persistent efforts for over two years and my letter with copies to Crown Prince Abdullah, the Saudi Washington Embassy was tired of this matter and decided to end even the annoyance of being bothered by our persistence. I have been told that the Saudis when confronted with a money problem first ignore the claim, then deny the claim, let the matter go to court and if they lose refuse to pay. Boy, if I only could do this with my obligations I wouldn't need to be paid for my services.

The First Secretary was his normal brilliant self in his letter. The first thing he did was to change completely what he asked me to do. Great strategy. By my responding to what he actually requested I failed to reply to what he did not request. Therefore there is no validity to my claim. The second strategy was to state I talked and responded to the wrong people who had no authority to solicit my services. Strategy three was to suggest I contact Dr. Clive Mohammed who he knew was dead. This is the Saudis way to settle a dispute. In my America we call it strike one, strike two, strike three, and you're OUT.

Unfortunately, First Secretary Al-Jubeir got a little careless and in the third paragraph he wrote:

"Several years ago, when you first contacted this Embassy, your claim was forwarded to the appropriate authorities in the Kingdom. At the time, the Minister of Information indicated that he knew of no agreement with you. I believe the American Embassy in Riyadh received the same response when it requested information on your behalf. I explained this to you in our telephone conversation."

H.R.H. Prince Bandar's April 13, 2000 letter to Congressman Boehlert had enclosed his assistant's letter to me plus the diplomatic note from his country to ours. He believed this was all that was ever needed. After all, the diplomatic note of March 1, 1999 stated that "The Ministry of Foreign Affairs wishes to advise the Embassy that the Ministry of Information has received NO correspondence from the above mentioned" (J.L. Dickson, Jr.). If the Kingdom of Saudi Arabia states they have received no correspondence from J.L. Dickson, Jr. prior to March 1, 1999 you can go to the bank with it. What difference does nine letters sent by either the Saudis or the U.S. State Department prior to March 1, 1999 have to do with anything. We certainly are not going to allow the Facts and Truth to interfere with the Saudi's Perception and Spin. What is the world coming to when the U.S. State Department cannot accept the Saudis written word. This is politics and you have a choice. Either believe what you see with your own eyes and know with your own intelligence, or believe what the Saudis tell you to believe. Just imagine how history would be changed if the facts were ever to be known, but it's not in the best interest of we people, all the little everyday people, to be told what we won't understand and what would create negative fall out. It is called diplomacy and truth is often sacrificed for diplomacy.

On May 1, 2000 I responded to First Secretary's letter of April 13, 2000. My letter was three pages and straight forward. I was stuck with Facts and Truth and I had little chance to be successful in the world of politics. All we little people believe in Santa Claus and the Tooth Fairy, so I kept repeating what I did and whom I did it for. All the time hoping for that miracle that every once in a while happens.

May 1, 2000

Dear Mr. Al-Jubeir:

Thank you for your letter of April 12, 2000.

Please allow me to respond to your letter and refresh your memory of our conversation on the one and only phone call we have ever had, although I have called you many, many times and have sent numerous correspondence to both you and Prince Bandar without receiving a reply.

There is no written contract. That point was made very clear in our conversation. You asked me to write to Minister Ali Al-Shair and refresh his memory by a time-line of events. This I did in my letter addressed to him, dated February 23, 1999. I mailed both the letter to him and a letter to you, also dated February 23, 1999, to your attention to forward to him by Special Embassy mailing, per your request. My letter to you states very clearly what I was to do, and does not support your comment in your April 12, 2000 letter.

In our conversation you agreed I did the work but that there was no proof it was done at the request of King Fahd and Minister Al-Shair. This conclusion, you stated, was based on the fact that you were in charge of the public relations project and my name was not listed with the Chancellor of Germany, high profile American politicians and other American VIP's, all soliciting your business.

A few reasons my name was not on your list are:
1. I didn't want to do a project of this magnitude and the sacrifices were very serious.
2. I would not be permitted to continue my consulting services as this project would take all my time. Because of the time differences many days would be sixteen hours long and a few would be even longer.
3. I would be required to move to Washington, D.C., the crime capital of America.

I was hesitant to accept the first two times I was asked to do the project, but I finally agreed if some very specific terms could be agreed on. Length of the project, compensation, and whom I would report to were critical to me. Minister Al-Shair agreed on the terms and my employment began.

As to the conversations with Embassy employees with no authority to commit the Saudi Government, the facts support that Second Secretary Abdulrahman A. Al-Shaia had the authority and exercised it on a daily basis. It was part of his job responsibility. Not only did he have authority, but in my case he was acting on orders from Minister Al-Shair, who gave him my name and phone number and instructed him to have me rush the completion of my proposal and deliver it to the Embassy as soon as possible. After many phone calls back and forth I was instructed by the Second Secretary to finish my proposal and deliver it to the Embassy by February 6, 1991.

This I did, accompanied by Dr. Clive Mohammed and Dr. Soraya Mashat, both representing Minister Al-Shair. Dr. Mashat was a long time and trusted employee of Minister Al-Shair, who was sent by him to work in the Embassy and reported to him on a regular basis.

Dr. Mashat kept me informed on the progress of the approval of the proposal and wanted to be a part of phase two. She called both me and my attorney many times, with comments, questions, and to advise what was needed to move the process at a faster pace. A letter she sent me with her Vita attached, dated September 17, 1991, was sent to you on April 30, 1999 as further proof of my employment with Minister Al-Shair.

How can you deny that my employment for Minister Al-Shair was not authorized by him when the Second Secretary, who reported to you, called me with knowledge of my name, phone number, and the exact nature of the project I was doing for both King Fahd and Minister Al-Shair?

Where did the Second Secretary get my name? Why would he take such risks? Isn't it obvious that Dr.

Clive Mohammed, a personal friend of Minister Al-Shair, had no reason to do what you claim?

Add to this that Dr. Mashat held many positions of authority for the Kingdom of Saudi Arabia over many years and was employed by Minister Al-Shair. She was the political advisor for the Ministry of Information in Jeddah, the Director of English Services of Radio Jeddah, the Information Officer for the Royal Embassy of Saudi Arabia Information Office in Washington D.C., and held many other positions of authority and responsibility.

Why would she call me many times at Minister Al-Shair's request with progress reports and with questions? One time she called expressly to expedite my answers to three questions King Fahd needed answered before he gave his final approval. The answers to these three questions were sent to King Fahd on May 26, 1991 and shortly thereafter he approved the proposal, and then the budget process began.

The answers to all the questions about why I did the work we both agree I did, and who I worked for, must be obvious by now. What is not obvious is why I have not been paid and why the denial. A better question might be why would the Kingdom of Saudi Arabia not extend to this American citizen the same courtesies extended to business people all over the world.

For additional proof the list of events I stated in my correspondence of February 23, 1999, can be easily verified by telephone records. My February 6, 1991 trip to the Saudi Embassy can be verified by records I signed to be admitted inside the Embassy and by a document from the Embassy that became a part of my proposal, given to me after I completed a survey on how the Embassy handled Public Relations.

Your suggestion that I contact Dr. Clive Mohammed is not possible as Dr. Al-Mashat informed me that he committed suicide.

This is a serious matter and my family and I have suffered economically, not only from monies not paid, but also from time and monies I paid to do the work King Fahd and Minister Al-Shair hired me to do.

The facts are clear. Let us meet and conclude this matter in a friendly and business-like manner. I have paid an enormous price to do the work I did. It is not too much to hope that the Kingdom of Saudi Arabia will honor their commitment.

Sincerely,
James L. Dickson, Jr.

Congressman Boehlert wrote again on May 2, 2000 and stated he was waiting on feedback from the Department of State. Why, I wondered. Didn't he catch on that the DOS would faithfully fulfill their obligation to the Saudis by endorsing one hundred percent of whatever they were told by the Kingdom? You either tote the party line or go out in the cruel world outside of government. I guess he was still an optimist, for on May 24, 2000, Barbara Larkin, Assistant Secretary, Legislative Affairs, Department of State replied and stated what was predicted. Paragraph four of the Assistant Secretary's letter said:

"Mr. Al-Jubeir wrote to Mr. Dickson that he found no documentation 'indicating the existence of any agreement between you and any entity of the Saudi government.' Mr. Dickson has previously stated that he will not pursue his claim under the Saudi legal system, and that he hoped the Embassy would recognize the validity of his claim. In these circumstances, the Department is unable to pursue this matter any further with the Saudi government. We regret that our reply cannot be more encouraging."

For a short time I was insulted that my government only needed a sentence from a Saudi Ambassador's Assistant to totally 'write me off'. Not only do they pretend to believe the Saudis, but also they would not, and still have not even given me a chance for a meeting to explain my case. This posture that an American citizen cannot even be given a hearing is counter to all we Americans believe is our right under the law and under our form of Democracy. Even the

Congressman was affected by this point of view and on June 12, 2000 he wrote to the Assistant Secretary, Legislative Affairs, Barbara Larkin. He told her about his 'lengthy personal meeting' with me in his district office. His letter was bold for a member of Congress even though he allowed some 'wiggle' room.

June 12, 2000

Dear Ms. Barbara:

Following receipt of your May 24, 2000 letter pertaining to the case of my constituent, James L. Dickson, Jr., President of J.L. Dickson Associates, in his dispute with the government of Saudi Arabia, I had a lengthy personal meeting with Mr. Dickson in my district office.

I came away from that meeting convinced that this case demands further consideration and consequently am formally requesting your assistance in setting up a meeting with the appropriate person(s) within the State Department to hear out Mr. Dickson. (David Sullivan?).

The lengthy presentation from Mr. Dickson to me led me to the conclusion that there are a great many coincidences and much circumstantial evidence to prompt a reasonable assumption that there is legitimacy to Mr. Dickson's claim that he was given the go-ahead to implement a plan to benefit the government of Saudi Arabia and that he was not compensated for the work. Who precisely gave the O.K. to do the work and what the stipulations and expectations were is an open question.

The bottom line is that I feel that Mr. Dickson is not letting his imagination run wild and that he is deserving further consideration of his case by the appropriate official(s) of our government.

I am anxious for your reaction.

Sincerely,
Sherwood Boehlert

While waiting for a response to Congressman Boehlert's letter to Barbara Larkin of the DOS, I received a reply from Adel Al-Jubeir in his response to my straightforward letter of May 1, 2000 to him. His June 20, 2000 letter did not disappoint me, for he continued to be consistent and tell the same story of his first letter, only he added a new creation, which was in our only conversation of over two years earlier he denied telling me that he agreed I did the work. Isn't it amazing that one year earlier I knew what he was going to write on the future date, and wrote my letter of February 23, 1999 where I stated exactly what he said and requested me to do? What magic I must have that I could tell the future so well. If truth must be known I wrote exactly what he requested. Not only did I do this but I called David Sullivan because I believed the First Secretary's request for me to write what I did for King Fahd and Minister Al-Shair and send the letter to him was a smokescreen, and what he really wanted was to find out why he and his boss Prince Bandar were not part of this decision to hire me. After all, he, Al-Jubeir, was the only person to handle all the twenty plus Public Relations Proposals and he had never heard of me.

His letter irritated me. I was tired of the game he was playing. Lack of income will sometimes force you to be more direct, so I wrote the following letter to Prince Bandar and enclosed my May 1, 2000 letter to Al-Jubeir. In this letter I stressed again the contradiction (100% error) contained in their diplomatic note and boldly asked for a one hour meeting so we could arrive at a mutual decision and that I was more than willing to travel to Washington and meet him at the Embassy so he would not be the least bit inconvenienced. Of course, my presenting irrefutable evidence to support my claim is and was the last item he would want to see. Much better to ignore my claim and allow the U.S. Department of State to take care of the problem for him. He knew he was far more important to the Department of State than any average American. The Saudis have much experience in dispute over claims and are experts in ways to handle them. In this case they went back to strategy one, ignore all inquiries and to this date I have not heard from anyone from the Kingdom of Saudi Arabia.

July 9, 2000

Your Royal Highness:

Please find enclosed a copy of the letter I sent to your assistant, First Secretary Adel Al-Jubeir, dated May 1, 2000 in response to his letter of April 12, 2000. The First Secretary made the following points in his letter:

1. He wanted me to forward to him a signed contract between either King Fahd or Minister Ali Al-Shair and myself.
2. That the conversation between me and Second Secretary Abdulrahman Al-Shaia and Dr. Soraya Al-Mashat did not commit the Embassy.
3. To contact Dr. Clive Mohammed and settle this matter directly with him.
4. That several years ago he contacted the Minister of Information and he did not know J.L. Dickson and that the U.S. State Department had the same response from their request.

My letter of May 1, 2000 covers each of these points, as follows:

1. He did not request me to forward a signed contract because he knew there was no written contract. We had discussed this at great length. He did ask me to write Minister Al-Shair to refresh his memory and send the

93

      correspondence to him for mailing by the Embassy to the Minister.

2. The Second Secretary called me and claimed he had the authority, plus he was acting for Minister Al-Shair, who had called the Embassy and requested that I finish the proposal as soon as possible and deliver the proposal to the Second Secretary at the Embassy for immediate delivery to him as King Fahd was waiting on it.
3. Dr. Al-Mashat informed me that Dr. Mohammed had committed suicide.

In your letter to Congressman Sherwood Boehlert, dated April 13, 2000 you made the point of sending him a copy of the diplomatic note sent by the Saudi Arabian Ministry of Foreign Affairs that stated "the Ministry of Information has received NO correspondence from the above mentioned." This is direct contradiction as evidenced by the third paragraph of the April 12, 2000 letter from the First Secretary:

"Several years ago, when you first contacted the Embassy, your claim was forwarded to the appropriate authorities in the Kingdom. At this time, the Minister of Information indicated that he knew of no agreement with you. I believe the American Embassy in Riyadh received the same response when it requested information on your behalf. I explained this to you in our telephone conversation."

The First Secretary is accurate on this point. He did convey that message to me. The question is, if several years ago they received correspondence about me from your Embassy, the U.S. State Department and several directly from me, why several years later in diplomatic note, can they claim they have received "NO correspondence" related to me. My letter of April 26, 1999 sent to the First Secretary was only about his inconsistency and stated the dates of correspondence sent to the Kingdom on many occasions and by several sources.

I'm aware that this matter is of far more importance to me and is but one of many, many items that cross the First Secretary's desk, and it would be easy for him not to recall all the information received and thereby understandable he had overlooked the important proof of the legitimacy of my employment to the Kingdom.

There are other points of inconsistency in correspondence from the First Secretary wherein I could prove my employment to the Kingdom, if given an opportunity to present this evidence directly to you for your consideration. One hour of your time would clear up all the inconsistencies and allow us to settle this matter quickly. I am more than willing to travel to Washington and meet with you at your convenience.

Haven't I earned a one hour meeting with you on the strength of thirty months of dedicated service to the Kingdom of Saudi Arabia? Will you please give me this opportunity to explain in detail what I did and first hand check all the evidence of my efforts so we can arrive at a mutual decision?

Sincerely,

James L. Dickson
President
J.L. Dickson Associates

I was still not ready to give up, so I decided to continue my efforts to have Hillary Clinton help me. It was now a good bet she would be New York's Junior Senator, and with a simple phone call to the right people she could do more in five minutes than I have been able to do in almost ten years. On August 19, 2000, after waiting for over a year for her to respond to my first letter, I wrote to her again. This time I was careful and made sure her name was spelled correctly.

August 19, 2000

Dear Hillary:

Please find enclosed a copy of the letter I wrote to you on July 31, 1999 asking for your help. As of this date there has been no response, so I choose to assume that none of your staff thought a letter from an average New Yorker was worthy of consideration. Hopefully they will take a different view this time.

Being a New York Senator is not easy. Helping your constituents is a big part of the job and sometimes it is not very rewarding. As a consultant for two governors I experienced first hand the many aspects and the endless requests for help from a wide variety of people. It is with this background that I understand the problem I have in getting your attention, and would not be wasting your time if I did not believe your help would solve this most important issue and solve it very quickly.

It is not possible to judge and or solve my problem with the Kingdom of Saudi Arabia by reading all the correspondence from all the sources. My Congressman, Sherwood Boehlert, took this approach and was not sure that he could help. After a personal meeting he changed his position 100% and sent a letter, enclosed, to Barbara Larkin of the State Department.

For me to be successful I need a personal meeting where I can explain and show proof for the work I did for almost three years. I have tried phone calls and correspondence but the complexities are difficult to explain without me, especially when the adversary is as clever as the Saudis and has a long record to support this conclusion.

Also enclosed are letters from Congressman Boehlert to Secretary of State Albright and my last letter to HRH Prince Bandar dated July 9th, 2000. Congressman Boehlert requested a meeting for me with the State Department but again there has been no reply. He is following this up with a phone call. I am not optimistic as the last three years have taught me I am not important enough for the State Department to meet with, but if they don't respond to the American people and don't respond to a member of Congress what is their function? Why should taxpayer dollars support their employment?

My frustration is starting to show. Other than Congressman Boehlert and his District Director Jean Donalty, no one in my government will give me the time of day. My Senator's office in Syracuse, Washington and New York have not returned over a dozen phone calls. The State Department, at my level of contact, can only write letters that are not effective. Is it any wonder so many Americans believe their government is not available to them and it exists only for the benefit and use of the elite few, and that voting is a wasted effort, for the average American is not represented by his elected official. Senator John McCain's message comes through loud and clear.

Hopefully you will start a new trend and represent all of the people and pre election promises will be followed by post election action. But I need your help now. Just one hour of your time. If that becomes a problem will you at very least help me to have a meeting in Washington with someone in authority at the State Department, and have a member of your staff represent you at the meeting and report back to you.

Thank you in advance for caring. Someone has to if we are to keep the American dream alive.

Sincerely,
J.L. Dickson, Jr.

The results were the same. The First Lady was much too important to waste her time responding to this New Yorker. I knew this, but was hoping that one of her many associates would at the very least send me regrets, and then when she won the election and became a New York Senator, I might be able to have better luck than I did with Senator Chuck Schumer. Her campaign was spinning how much she wanted to help the people of New York, and you never know when someone running for elected office might keep a few of their campaign promises. Obviously I was much too much an optimist and didn't at this time really understand how little individual effort is spent on any one person. I guess I wasn't looking at the bigger picture and should have known better for the history of President Clinton left a lot of broken people along the way. It's the same story, some people are more equal than all the rest of us. I'm learning, but it's leaving a bitter taste in my mouth and a lot less respect for people in government.

All was not lost for Congressman Boehlert was still determined to help me. But, the Congressman received a letter from Barbara Larkin that closed the door in his being able to help me. This letter from him has been the last letter I have received from his office. They tried and tried hard to help but their resources are not enough to overcome the magical relationship America has with the Kingdom of Saudi Arabia. Sherwood Boehlert, a New York Congressman, will always have my thanks and my vote. He was the only member of Congress to really give a damn. It is not his fault the U.S. State Department has more important matters than helping individual Americans and that the Secretary of State is so important, she, Madeleine Albright, cannot take the time to respond to even a Member of Congress. His letter to me and Barbara Larkin's letter to him are printed below in their entirety. They represent what this book is about and tell the story of my failure to have anyone in authority even want to find out what took place. As stated before, people do things for their own reasons and those in power take care of only those who help them stay in power. Constituent services are two words that are part of a candidate for elected office's public relations program and have no meaning in the real world that most of us live in.

September 7, 2000

Dear Mr. Dickson:

I am enclosing a copy of this letter I received from Ms. Larkin in response to my most recent inquiry on your behalf.

As you will note, Ms. Larkin states the Department of State (DoS) has exhausted all options it has at this point in representing your claim with Saudi officials. She indicates that until you have exercised available legal action and/or have additional information to submit for consideration, the department can do nothing further to assist you. Based upon the current situation, Ms. Larkin confirms that the department's position is that there would be no benefit to a personal meeting with the DoS staff.

In addition to my written correspondence to DoS, I have spoken with Ms. Larkin and indicated my interest in and support of your efforts to resolve your claim. However, the department continues to maintain its staff has done everything it can do to represent your interests.

I sincerely regret this response could not have been more in line with your wishes. I know the amount of time and energy you put into the project itself and efforts to process your claim.

You may keep me updated on any further action you take and as appropriate, I will do what I can to represent your interests.

With warmest regards,

Sincerely,

Sherwood Boehlert
Ms. Larkin's letter:

James L. Dickson Jr.

August 21, 2000

Dear Mr. Boehlert,

Thank you for your letter of June 12, concerning the claim against Saudi Arabia of your constituent, James L. Dickson, President of J.L. Dickson Associates. We apologize for the delay in responding.

As you are aware from several exchanges of correspondence, the Department has worked with Mr. Dickson at length to assist him in pursuing his claim. Since June 1998, the Department has contacted the Saudi Embassy in Washington numerous times, both orally and in writing, on Mr. Dickson's behalf, to provide documents for him and to press for a response. Furthermore, the U.S. Embassy in Riyadh has contacted the Saudi government, transmitted documents from Mr. Dickson, and requested consideration and a response from the Saudi Ministry of Information.

The Saudi Government responded to our Embassy in Riyadh in March 1999, calling Mr. Dickson's claim "completely groundless" as far as records of the Ministry of Information are concerned. An official of the Saudi Embassy in Washington responded in April 2000, stating that he found no documentation "indicating the existence of any agreement between [Mr. Dickson] and any entity of the Saudi government."

We share Mr. Dickson's disappointment with these conclusions. However, as indicated in the Department's letter to you of May 24, the Department is not in a position to pursue this matter any further with the Saudi government, given that Saudi officials have denied the validity of Mr. Dickson's claim, that he has elected not to pursue his claim in Saudi or U.S. courts, and that he has chosen to seek compensation solely by requesting it from Saudi officials.

100

Under generally accepted principles of international law and longstanding State Department practice, the U.S. government can only consider espousing, or formally adopting as its own, a private claim against another government if three prerequisites are met: (1) the claim involves a violation of the state's international responsibilities; (2) the claimant was a U.S. citizen at the time of the claim arose and continually thereafter to the date of espousal; (3) the claimant has exhausted available local legal remedies. Because Mr. Dickson has not met the third of these requirements, the United States is not in a position to espouse his claim against the Saudi Government.

Moreover, since any presentation or argument of Mr. Dickson's claim would be conducted primarily in writing, it would be best for any additional arguments, evidence, or materials that Mr. Dickson may have to be submitted to the Department in writing, rather than in a personal meeting. We have invited him to provide any such additional materials for our consideration. If appropriate, we will arrange for Department officials to transmit any new materials to Saudi authorities on his behalf. If at any time we believe that a meeting with Mr. Dickson would be helpful to our consideration of his claim, we will proceed to arrange such a meeting.

With these considerations in mind, the extensive steps taken by the Department on Mr. Dickson's behalf are all that it appropriately can do at this time. In light of the negative responses from the Saudi Government, there would be no benefit to Mr. Dickson to arranging for him to meet with Department officials. We regret that this reply cannot be more encouraging.

Sincerely,
Barbara Larkin

Assistant Secretary
Legislative Affairs

After reading the letter from Barbara Larkin I wasn't sure if I should get sick or mad. Mad won out and I called David Sullivan. I reminded him of our last phone conversation where he assured me he was able and capable to make a decision to have a meeting one on one with me in Washington, and that he was not permitted to do so. So much for a good education, a law degree and a good job in the State Department when you're not able to exercise your judgment and have the freedom to even have one meeting with the person you're trying to help. What a system! The next topic was Barbara Larkin's letter and I started with a simple question. "Do you, David Sullivan, know of cases where the American businessman took the Saudi businessman to court, won the case, and were never paid?" His answer was yes. Next question. "Can you name a case where the American businessman after winning the case the Saudis actually paid the American?" He couldn't remember. Last question. "If the Saudis are not required and or do not pay if they lose in court, are there any competent attorneys who would exercise this option and waste their time unless they were paid for their services up front?" There was no need for him to answer, for we both knew of cases won in court but the winner didn't collect any monies, so the Barbara Larkin letter stating the generally accepted perception of international law was first a State Department's way of saying please don't bother us again. Her second point that a meeting would not be in their best interest as any presentation I might make would (not could) be conducted primarily in writing. What a joke. The truth comes out loud and clear when she states that the Saudi Government called my claim "completely groundless" and a Saudi official (Adel Al-Jubeir) stated he found no documentation "indicating the existence of any agreement". Let's be clear about what is stated here. In straight language what Barbara Larkin is saying, if the Saudis say it isn't so then it isn't so, and don't bother to try to impress us with any proof because the Saudi word will transcend any and all proof. Our decision is final and let's go on to the next case, thank you very much.

Some people don't know when to quit. I was close to giving up, but had one more battle plan. Sure, it was a long shot and I had wasted enough time in my optimistic naivety, but it was now about a lot more than money. It was really about time I started winning. I would try again.

CHAPTER NINE

The start of the new century did not bring about any changes in Congress. There wasn't any 'new' beginnings, despite the New Year and New Century resolutions to the contrary. My New Year's resolution was to bring the project to a close. So without a lot of hope, I wrote a letter to Senator John McCain on January 22, 2001. His campaign finance plan was to take some of the fantastic sums of money given to Members of Congress out of politics. This, he carefully explained, would give the average American a better opportunity to be represented by the people they had voted into office, and the democracy the founding fathers had envisioned just might catch on. Imagine, we the people were going to be represented by our elected officials! This sounded like Dr. Martin Luther King's "I Have a Dream" program, and sometimes dreams do come true.

Senator McCain did not answer. There was no letter from a staff member informing me that he would like to help but an Arizona Senator has all he can do to help his own constituents. The cold hard reality of today was to be the same as it was yesterday and that means there was more work for me to do.

Foolish but still determined, I decided to try one more time to get help from my now Senator, Hillary Clinton. My January 24, 2001 letter to her was short and to the point. Of course I reminded her of my previous letters. This was to be my last effort to a member of Congress. My philosophy was, if you fail, pick yourself up and try again. You only need to win once to wipe out the negativity of all the failures. Remember you can find a pot of gold only when you have the courage to follow the rainbow to its end. Hillary was to be the last rainbow I followed. It took a while, but the Junior New York Senator finally answered.

Five months later, on May 30, 2001, I received a one-paragraph letter from Hillary telling me she had assigned a Constituent Liaison to handle my case. The next day I received a copy of the letter the Senator wrote to Ms. Roxanne Reed of the U.S. Department of State, that instructed her to reply to Hillary's New York office to the attention of Jennifer Kritz. I quickly called Ms. Kritz and was given a one-hour appointment. Excited, I reviewed my material and made copies of all pertinent correspondence, and placed a table of contents in the package as there were so many pages from so many different people, and it could be confusing. The correspondence represented years of data and was from two Senators, members of the U.S. Department of State, Congressman Boehlert, Prince Bandar, First Secretary Al-Jubeir, the diplomatic note and much of my correspondence to all of the above.

I arranged the material I would present and then timed how long it would take me to present a concise story. When I could do it in forty minutes I knew I was prepared as anyone could be to explain such a complex project in such a short period of time.

This was it. I had my last chance to settle my case and I was determined to put my best foot forward and let the facts represent me. My appointment with Jennifer Kritz was scheduled for 11:30 a.m. on June 13, 2001, but she was too busy that day and said she could see me for at least one hour on June 14, 2001 if I could get there by 11 a.m. That was no problem and I started for New York at 4 a.m. with my wife and a business friend who was very familiar with the project and all my efforts. It was like going to the most important meeting of your life, and fighting for your economic survival. The three of us went around and around on what I would say and how strong I would say it. The miles flew by and we arrived in New York just before 10 a.m. and found a garage near the Senator's office. My wife took a taxi to visit a relative dying of cancer, and my friend and I arrived at 780 Third Avenue around 10:30. A call from security in the building was placed to the Senator's office and we were told we were too early and no, we could not come to Suite 2601 and wait, due to security. We tried to enter a little later and were finally permitted to go to the reception room and wait until a busy Jennifer Kritz could see us.

An assistant of Jennifer came out and escorted us to a meeting room. Jennifer finally arrived, and after she made several phone calls we started our meeting. The first few minutes were spent trying to educate Jennifer as fully as time would allow. I knew to be effective that Senator Clinton's Constituent Liaison agent had to carry the ball for me and Jennifer had to, with some accuracy and conviction, represent me. I had learned it was difficult enough to have a meeting with a Congressional Aid and that I should not expect a member of Congress to actually meet with a person of my economic and political status. This was, in the real world, the best I could hope for.

Poor Jennifer Kritz. She was willing, but interruptions were a part of her day. We prevailed and though I rushed through the presentation, all my major points were presented. Plus, I left her with all the written material up to that time so she could 'get the feel' of what was real and true. She listened with interest but didn't have time to ask any questions. When the meeting was over, she promised to read all the material and be my advocate. Who could ask for more?

On the way back home, my business companion expressed his opinion on how the meeting went. He was confident that only positives could come from the meeting but worried if Jennifer had the time to fully explain what was given to her. She appeared to be wearing more than one hat and had more on her schedule than one person could devote much time to. There are so many people asking for help and not enough people to adequately be able to do the job they would like to do. The drive back went quickly and it was agreed that this sixteen-hour day had been a success.

After waiting almost three months, I wrote a follow up letter to Jennifer with a copy to the Senator. I was tired of waiting for a reply, so I called several times to get in touch with Ms. Kritz over the phone. Every time I called, there was no response on the other end. I left a few voicemails, but that is as far as I got. Sounds familiar doesn't it?

August 13, 2001

Dear Jennifer:

It has been eight weeks since you and I met in Senator Clinton's New York office. I have tried to call you several times without success and left you messages on two of the calls. On my last call I was transferred to a recording that stated how busy the Senator's office is and to be patient waiting for a return call. I understand this, so I though it best to reach you by letter.

Please reply and let me know:

105

-Have you read the material I left with you?

-Has the State Department replied to the Senator's letter of May 30, 2001?

-Have you taken any action in my regards?

Again, thank you for our June 14, 2001 meeting and the interest the Senator and you have in helping me solve this very serious problem. Senator Clinton, as you know, is one of a few people in government that can bring this matter directly to the 'right' people. Without her help, and the attention her help creates, there is little opportunity for me to be paid for over thirty-one months of work I did for King Fahd and Minister Al-Shair of the Kingdom of Saudi Arabia.

It seems that the Kingdom of Saudi Arabia, because of American oil needs, have a special status and that the State Department doesn't wish to "rock the boat". Therefore, at the suggestion of my Congressman, I'm writing a book detailing this project and all of my efforts to be paid for my work.

Sincerely,
J.L. Dickson, JR

P.S, Thought that you might be interested in an exciting new development in my book that has occurred since our meeting. Currently two publishing firms have requested and been sent the preface and the first two chapters of my book, and one publisher was interested in my ability to go on the talk circuit and college campuses to promote the book. The theme being, this is what can and what does happen in the "real" world to "real" people and as stated in my book, that those in power only have time for those who help them stay in power.

Finally on October 2, 2001 Jennifer wrote me a letter and the last sentence stated, "Please be assured that Senator Clinton's office has done all it possibly can to assist you and that your case has received a thorough review."

Just imagine all the work they did for me:
- My third letter was finally answered and the State Department was requested to comment.
- I had a one-hour meeting in New York City with the Constituent Liaison.
- Four months later I received a letter from Senator Clinton's New York office, but without the enclosed State Department's letter actually being enclosed. Take note that the State Department's letter was sent to Senator Clinton's office on June 25, 2001 and received by the office on June 29, 2001. It took over three months to mail that letter to me.
- After waiting for five weeks and making several unsuccessful phone calls to the New York office, I called the Senator's Washington office and requested I be sent the State Department's letter as promised. Several weeks later I received the letter from the State Department without any correspondence from the Washington sender, but attached to the State Department's letter was a printed message. How impersonal can you possibly be? The letter from Paul Kelly, Assistant Secretary, Legislative Affairs, Department of State stated exactly what Barbara Larkin stated. How original.

Is this really all the Junior Senator from New York could do for me? I found it very disappointing that she wrote a short note to the Department of State and when the Assistant Secretary, Legislative Affairs Office responded that his department could not help and the Department of State had done all it could for J.L. Dickson, she had Jennifer Kritz write me a letter stating her office had also done all it possible could to help me. Give me a break! I'm not asking to be treated like the people were treated at the end of Bill Clinton's term in office, the Dicksons won't be sending contributions to the library fund or employing any family relatives to help move this project to a favorable conclusion. What I was seeking was some old fashion constituent service similar to what Sherry Boehlert and his staff offered. Is that request too much to expect? How about having a staff member to read and respond to the material I left at her New York office, or at the very least, someone in her office could have responded to my one page letter. How sad, the greatest country on earth has time and money for so many causes and countries, but can't find the time to help the people at home. Chris Matthews, where are you when you're needed?

So I give up seeking to be paid for over thirty one months work for the King and a Minister of the Kingdom of Saudi Arabia. I'm not the first or last that has suffered this fate. No more attempts to be paid, but I will try to bring the experience and knowledge gained from this project to the public in the hope that others will benefit.

CHAPTER TEN

Because so much has happened due to the Gulf War and our continued occupation with military in the Kingdom of Saudi Arabia, a last chapter will conclude this work with an up-to-date of what has happened to some of the people I was involved with. Although there are some events I'm not willing to make public, most of what I know, because of this project, has been reported. It is a personal belief that if the Public Relations Project had gone forward, by me or someone more expert than me, the conflict we are now so deeply involved in might have been prevented. If this sounds like positive posturing on my part, please forgive me for my continued optimistic dreaming.

This book is about so much more than money and what happened to one person. It is a reflection of government's lack of ethics and values. Sound bites replace dialogue and the public is not fully informed. In all my travels and efforts, with the exception of Congressman Boehlert and his District Director Jean Donalty, the people I contacted were more interested in finding a reason not to help me than in taking the time to become acquainted with the facts and then proceeding to do their job. It would be too negative to bring all my experiences where I was politely and sometimes not so politely dismissed, but two examples from the U.S. Department of State will be enough to paint the story accurately.

    a.   I wanted to thank Barbara Larkin for her first letter to Congressman Boehlert and was given her phone number by his office. After being asked who I was and what I wanted, I was told that this office of the U.S. Department of State was not for the American public and if they actually connected me to Ms. Larkin's office they would have been fired. I thanked the person and made the comment that I was surprised that public dollars were used to fund a department of government, and the people who pay their salaries and huge benefits are not permitted to talk to anyone there.

    b.   I called Ginny Pratt at the Saudi Desk of the DOS and asked her for the number of her boss and his boss. I decided to place a call to the Deputy Assistant Secretary, Allen Keiswetter, and was advised that a Ms. Brown would connect me. I was informed on my first call by a gentleman that would not identify himself that the Office of the Deputy Assistant Secretary does not take calls from the American Public, and that's why they have the Saudi Desk. I placed a second call and asked for Ms. Brown. She told me she had never heard of me and could not pass my call to this very important person of the U.S. State Department. I reported both of these experiences to Jean Donalty at Congressman Boehlert's Utica office.

The experience from these two attempts to contact someone in a higher pay grade was repeated every time any attempts were made to move my case to a higher level. It did not matter if a member of Congress made the contact or if I made the contact. Congressman Boehlert wrote two letters to Secretary of State Albright and never received a reply from her. His request for a meeting in Washington between me and the Department of State people was refused. Senator D'Amato's two requests to then Ambassador Wyche Fowler resulted in the Ambassador suggesting I take my problems to attorneys in Saudi Arabia or in the U.S. He didn't care where I went as long as he wasn't involved and he could continue his relationship with the Saudis. In his second letter he stated, "Unfortunately, the U.S. Government cannot represent Mr. Dickson in his claim against the Saudi Government." Why not!? What is the function of an Ambassador if not to assist any American in the country where he, the Ambassador, has been assigned? Yes, I know, if the U.S. State Department helps every American, their popularity with the host country will suffer. Wyche Fowler didn't have to worry for he was popular with the Saudi Government and it's my best guess I wasn't important enough for him to risk upsetting the Royal Family. My case wasn't the first case that it has been suggested that this Ambassador valued his public relations with the host VIP's more than he valued his duty to the Americans that he was assigned to help.

Remember, this is the same Department of State that has replied to Congressman Boehlert on all their efforts to help me. They must all take the same class and are told how to respond to Americans asking for assistance. My favorite response was, "The Department of State's ready to provide ordinary consular assistance." It is so ordinary that only low level employees are permitted to help all of we 'ordinary people', for their job titles cannot even elicit a reply to their requests. My experience with the Department of State, on any level, has led me to the conclusion that the department is not set up for ordinary people with problems that 'need' help from someone in authority. That's why there are so many low level employees to handle the phone calls and write letters to other low level people. At this level, little progress is made.

A short chapter was written about Dr. Clive Mohammed, as he was the individual responsible for my taking this assignment. This story has a very sad ending. If you remember my letter to the Saudi Embassy, I stated that Dr. Soraya Al-Mashat had informed me that Dr. Clive had committed suicide. I'm not sure this is true. Without going into all the details (it would make a great TV movie) allow me to state simply: Dr. Clive Mohammed was finally accused of having his second wife killed. He was accused by his daughter, and the story made huge headlines both in Sarasota, Florida and in Puerto Rico. The details are available to all who care to become informed. The police and district attorney in Sarasota brought the man Dr. Clive stated he hired to kill his wife Irma to trial with the principle witness being Dr. Mohammed. After this man was acquitted Clive was charged and he was sentenced to the Marion C.I. Facility and was to be released on June 28, 2014. A check through the use of the computer states he is now deceased. What a horrible waste!

This story would not be complete without an update on First Secretary, Adel Al-Jubeir, Royal Saudi Arabia Embassy, Washington D.C. Mr. Al-Jubeir is now the Advisor to Crown Prince Abdullah and is seen often on many of our TV channels, most notably MSNBC's "Hardball with Chris Matthews". The First Secretary is an articulate, extremely well informed person of great talent. Unfortunately, his job was not to help me, but instead to carry the messages from people not interested in acknowledging the work I was hired to do for King Fahd and ex-Minister of Information, Ali Al-Shair. He was brilliant in his job to deny the truth about me and my employment. His only mistake was to, with one hundred percent accuracy, write two sentences in his first letter that by his own words prove what I did and who I did it for. Although he tried to correct one of these sentences in his next letter, it was too late and the 'cat was let out of the bag'. So much for the truth

111

when no one pays any attention to it. Both of the First Secretaries letters are part of this work.

His Royal Highness, Prince Bandar, finally answered the last letter Congressman Boehlert wrote to him. In it he sent a copy of the diplomatic note from his country to ours. It was a subtle way of stating that Saudi Arabia never heard of me and never received any correspondence from me, therefore there is no claim and that's the end of this case. It did not matter that Ambassador Fowler had letters from me, hand carried to him, or that Prince Bandar's assistant, First Secretary Al-Jubeir acknowledged my correspondence to the Embassy prior to the date on the diplomatic note. What is important to remember is that the Kingdom of Saudi Arabia states many times they haven't received any of my many correspondences and no matter how many times they received these letters, the official governmental response is, "Received NO correspondence from J.L. Dickson" and that is final. The Ambassador knows that the U.S. State Department knows which side of their bread is buttered and who butters it. So let's forget about truth and justice and go on to something important, for certainly the U.S. State Department understands that there are so much more important issues than what happens to one ordinary American. Again, Fact and Truth are held hostage by Perception and Spin, and it doesn't matter who knows it or who is embarrassed by it, for the world goes round and round on money and influence and what happens to all we little people is of no consequence.

To this "ordinary American" a diplomatic note from one country to another is important, very important. It tells a lot about the relationship between the two countries. The diplomatic note from the kingdom of Saudi Arabia on March 1, 1999 to the United States Department of State contained only inaccurate statements. Even one member of the U.S Department of State tried unsuccessfully to explain to me that 'No Correspondences' did not mean no correspondences. Honest! This employee created a scenario, a 'dialogue of explanation,' that in the end concluded that the word 'No' really meant 'not recently' and therefore the diplomatic note was totally accurate. I didn't know if I should be embarrassed by her loyalty to the Saudis or outraged by her attempts to influence me. I settled for being embarrassed and told her I would never bother her again and that she should get her priorities straight. After all she is an American. Little did I know at that point in time, the Saudis word was to be taken seriously and was the final position on the matter for all State Department employees. It was, and still is, difficult to understand that my country went to war to prevent the Iraqi's from invading Saudi Arabia and the Kingdom has no respect or love for Americans.

Somehow I have never caught up with the concept that only the elite few and the position they take are to be considered important enough to be taken seriously. I keep tripping over that each of us are to be treated equally and that justice is blind to the differences among us. It is this idealistic notion that separates most of us from those who understand and know how to play the game. No wonder election contributions are in the millions of dollars both to Congress and the President and elections are won and lost on who has the most money.

Now, a year after the horrific events of 9-11-01 America has learned much more about her Saudi ally. American's from all walks of life have come forward with their personal stories about what happened to them in both business and formal dealings. Each story is similar although the details are quite unique. A common thread is that the Saudis "Do as they please" with the assurance that the U.S State Department will back their play and members of congress will be helpless to render assistance to their constituents, even when they are so disposed to do so. It would appear that there are forces more powerful and more important than congress and the people that vote for them.

Justice and individual rights that most of us take for granted must take a back seat. We can only wonder why an aggressive media, eager to out-perform each other does not pursue, report and highlight more of these events. Without the media's help there is little opportunity that change will occur and the VIP's and the well connected will keep on exploiting us and will confound the experts on the question of the day; when is enough, enough?

We Americans need more information about this oil rich country and the "deals" between our governments. Experiences like mine, Patricia Roush, Saks Fifth Ave, etc.etc.etc, will serve as guidelines for those who follow us and are about to enter into any type of relationship with the Saudis. The publication of these experiences is a public service and will aid members of congress to be better prepared to serve their constituents. Add to this the addition of the voices of an informed public and the media will be better able to do their job and this in turn will aid the Kingdom of Saudi Arabia to finally enter the international world of the twenty-first century.

There is much work to be done and we better get to it quickly if we are ever to have peace in the Middle East and avoid American military presence in that part of the world for decades to come. It is time for the Saudis to step up to the plate and acknowledge their American ally and correct, where possible, the errors of the past. The outside world is catching on to them with stories like mine. What other country in the world would send an official diplomatic note from their Ministry of Foreign affairs to our American Embassy advising that their Ministry of Information has received NO CORRESPONDENCES from J.L Dickson, when they have received many, many correspondences that have been sent by their own Embassy, the United States Department of State, U.S ambassadors and members of the U.S Congress as well as by me.

In the back of the book is that Kingdom of Saudi Arabia's diplomatic note dated March 1, 1999 and some of the many correspondences that preceded it. This alone should have been enough for my government to take action, for it shows the incredible arrogance of the Saudis towards all of America. It also will illustrate better than all the words I have written, about the way our government treats it's own citizens and the position of the U.S Department of State to "ordinary" Americans doing business in this oil rich country.

The following correspondences were written, sent and received by the Saudis before they sent the diplomatic note of March 1, 1999:

I. Letter from J.L Dickson Associates to the Minister of Information Ali Al-Shair on January 22, 1998 that referenced (4) correspondences sent from attorney Joseph Siracusa offices dated July 30, 1991; January 1992; June 1992; August 1995.

II. Letter from Senator D'Amato to me dated January 28, 1998 with a copy of the letter from U.S Ambassador Wyche Fowler requesting I address correspondences to the new Minister of Information, His Excellency Faud Al–Salam, so the ambassador could forward the letter to the minister.

III. Letter from me dated March 9, 1998 to His Excellency, Minister Faud Al-Salam sent by Senator D'Amato with his letter to me dated March 24, 1998.

IV. Letter hand carried to His Royal Highness Prince Bandar by a friend who was going to a luncheon and meeting with him, dated May 13, 1998.

V. Letter from Congressman Sherwood Boehlert dated May 30, 1998 to me informing me he had sent letters on my behalf to the Department of State (DOS) in Washington and directly to the Saudi Embassy in Washington.

VI. Letter from the United States Department of State, attorney - advisor David B. Sullivan to me dated July 1, 1998 with cover letter from him to commercial attaché Abdullah Al-Athel that states:

"As I explained in our telephone conversation on June 30, 1998, I am forwarding the enclosed letter to the Ambassador, His Royal Highness Prince Bandar Bin Sultan from Mr. James L. Dickson Jr., a United States citizen and the President of J.L DICKSON ASSOCIATES. Mr. Dickson states that the government of Saudi Arabia owes him compensation for services rendered between 1990 & 1992".

VII. Letter from the United Sates Department of State, attorney - advisor David B. Sullivan to me dated December 11, 1998 telling me of a transmittal letter to the Embassy in Riyadh, Saudi Arabia. Enclosed with this letter was attorney Sullivan's transmittal letter dated November 10, 1998 to John Moran, Economic counselor, U.S Embassy, Riyadh, which stated:

"Enclosed, as described in a forthcoming cable, are two packets of materials concerning Mr. James Dickson. The first packet contains correspondence and information for forwarding to the Saudi Minister of Information. The second packet contains additional packets for your information only, which are not to be forwarded to the Saudi government. Please contact me if you have any questions. Thank you for your assistance.

Sincerely,
David B. Sullivan
Attorney - Advisor
For International Claims
& Investment Disputes

VIII. Letter from me dated February 23, 1999 to Adel Al-Jubeir, First Secretary (assistant to Ambassador Bandar bin Sultan) Saudi Embassy, Washington. This was the letter requested by First Secretary Al-Jubeir during my telephone conversation with him December 1997. Enclosed was my letter to His Excellency, Minister Al-Shair requested by first secretary Al-Jubeir and the correspondence he would send by diplomatic courier to the Minister for his response to my claim.

Adel Al-Jubeir stated he would respond to me on the reply from the Minister and if the Minister acknowledged that I was invited by the King to create a public relations project for the Kingdom, and that he, Al-Shair, was to direct me on this project, all monies owed to me would be paid at once.

IX. The closest to a reply I was ever to receive was the letter written by First Secretary Al-Jubier on April 20, 2002 to me, directed by His Royal Highness Prince Bandar. In that letter the third paragraph read:

"Several years ago, when you first contacted this Embassy, your claim was forwarded to the appropriate authorities in the Kingdom. At the time, the Minister of Information indicated that he knew of NO agreement with you. I believe the American Embassy in Riyadh received the same response when it requested information on your behalf. I explained that to you in our telephone conversation."

This statement is 100% accurate. It was a serious mistake the First Secretary made in stating it, for it contradicted the diplomatic note of NO CORRESPONDENCES of March 1, 1999. Several years ago meant they had stated in 1997 that they had never heard of me. For the record, they had not heard of me over nine times as evidenced by the above nine correspondences. There were many other letters written and sent by me that are not noted here, as I believe it is best to only use as proof what was done by U.S and Saudi Official Government people and agencies. Is it any wonder that my belief is, the U.S State Department holds the Saudi position on any matter to be their official position and that we "ordinary" Americans have little hope of finding truth and justice when we turn to them for help. They know who to support and who to sacrifice.

The U.S. State Department got this message a long time ago and their policy and practice supports it. It has taken me much longer to catch on. So I want to thank you for reading my story. Remember, in our America, the people's America, you and me together can make a difference. We still have our own right to vote and if we start to take part by making our voices and opinions known we can bring the democracy of yesterday into a better America today. The future is ours to shape and not the bureaucrats that believe that we are really not smart enough to kick them out of office, so lets work together to make our today's dreams become tomorrow's reality and to ensure that the promise of America's Democracy becomes available to all we 'everyday Americans' and not just the 'elite' few who rob us of our heritage.

A last word for the Kingdom of Saudi Arabia. I worked twelve to sixteen hour days proudly for you. But you took my work and DENIED my employment. I spent my retirement money to set up a Public Relations Project for you that would take you into the world community of the twenty-first century. But you DENIED me my fair and agreed on compensation. Shame on you! You really don't understand we Americans, especially we common everyday Americans. I wish you good luck and may today's tomorrows bring you peace and understanding in a world that will someday learn that the differences among us are not the reason we are in conflict, it is the greed and lack of humanity in the few guilty men that live among us.

DOCUMENTS USED IN THE BOOK

* February 6, 1991	Daily News Summery from survey Saudis Washington Embassy
* January 22, 1998	Letter from J.L. Dickson Jr, to Minister of Information Ali Al-Shair
* February 23, 1999	Letter from J.L. Dickson Jr, to Minister of Information Ali Al-Shair
* April 21, 1999	Letter from J.L. Dickson Jr, to First Secretary Al-Jubeir
* September 17, 1991	Letter from Dr. Soraya Mashat to J.L. Dickson Jr, with Vita
* December 7, 1999	Letter from J.L. Dickson Jr, to First Secretary Al-Jubeir
* February 24, 2000	Letter from Congressman Boehlert to Secretary of State Albright
* May 1, 2000	Letter from J.L. Dickson Jr, to First Secretary Al-Jubeir
* June 12, 2000	Letter from Congressman Boehlert to Assistant Secretary of State Barbara Larkin
* August 19, 2000	Letter from J.L. Dickson Jr, to First Lady Hillary Clinton

PARTIAL LISTING OF CORRESPONDENCES

* April 11, 1990	Dr. Clive I. Mohammed to J.L. DICKSON Jr.
* June 13, 1990	Congressman James T. Walsh to J.L. DICKSON Jr.
* March 9, 1998	J.L. DICKSON Jr. to Ambassador Wyche Fowler Jr.
* March 9, 1998	J.L. DICKSON Jr. to Minister Faud abd Al-Salam
* April 21, 1998	Ambassador Fowler to Senator Alfonse D'Amato with Fax
* May 13, 1998	J.L. DICKSON Jr. to His Royal Highness Prince Bandar
* May 30, 1998	Congressman Sherwood Boehlert to J. L. DICKSON Jr
* July 2, 1998	DoS Attorney-Advisor David B. Sullivan to J.L. DICKSON Jr. with his letter to Commercial Attache, Saudi Embassy, Abdul Al-Athel.
* December 11, 1998	DoS Attorney- Advisor David B. Sullivan to John Moran, U.S. Embassy Riyadh
* March 12, 1999	DoS Attorney-Advisor David B. Sullivan to J.L. DICKSON Jr. with Diplomatic Note
* February 23, 1999	J.L. DICKSON Jr. to First Secretary Adel Al-Jubeir
* April 26, 1999	J.L. DICKSON Jr. to First Secretary Adel Al-Jubeir
* May 20, 1999	Congressman Boehlert to J.L. DICKSON Jr.
* July 31, 1999	J.L. DICKSON Jr. to Hillary Clinton
* August 6, 1999	Congressman Boehlert to J.L. DICKSON Jr.

* September 16, 1999	Congressman Boehlert to J.L. DICKSON Jr. with letter from Assistant Secretary of DoS Barbara Larkin
* January 7, 2000	Congressman Bohlert to J.L. DICKSON Jr. with his letter to H.R.H. Prince Bandar bin Sultan
* Febraury 14, 2000	Congressman Boehlert to Secretary of State Madeleine K. Albright
* March 22, 2000	Congressman Boehlert to Secretary of State Madeleine K. Albright
* April 3, 2000	Congressman Boehlert to H.R.H. Prince Bandar bin Sultan
* April 12, 2000	First Secretary Adel Al-Jubeir, Saudi Embassy in Washington D.C., to J.L. DICKSON Jr.
* May 2, 2000	Congressman Boehlert to J.L. DICKSON Jr. with letter from H.R.H. Prince Bandar bin Sultan bin Abdulaziz
* June 12, 2000	Congressman Boehlert to J.L. DICKSON Jr. with his letter to Assistant Secretary DoS Barbara Larkin and her letter to the Congressman
* June 20,2000	First Secretary Adel Al-Jubeir, Saudi Embassy in Washington D.C., to J.L. DICKSON Jr.
* July 9, 2000	J.L. DICKSON Jr. to H.R.H. Prince Bandar bin Sultan
* September 7, 2000	Congressman Boehlert to J.L. DICKSON Jr. with letter from DoS Assistant Secretary Barbara Larkin
* January 24, 2001	J.L. DICKSON Jr. to Senator Hillary Clinton
* May 30, 2001	Senator Hillary Clinton to J.L. DICKSON Jr.
* October 2, 2001	Jennifer Kritz, Constituent Laison for Senator Clinton with letter dated June 25, 2001 from DoS Assistant Secretary Paul V. Kelly

Dr. Clive I. Mohammed

CHIEF, DENTAL SERVICES
ARMED FORCES HOSPITAL

DR. CLIVE I. MOHAMMED
KING FAHD ARMED FORCES HOSPITAL
P.O.BOX 9862,
JEDDAH 21159
SAUDI ARABIA

APRIL 11, 1990

MR. JAMES L. DICKSON, JR. PRESEDENT,
J.L. DICKSON ASSOCIATES
P.O.BOX 271
HAMILTON
NEW YORK 13346

Dear Jim,

It was indeed a pleasure talking with you recently and I have again
enclosed a copy of a memo of understanding which was discussed
previously. I have had another original prepared since somehow
the one sent previously was not delivered.

I would again like to take this opportunity to express our
appreciation for your very kind hospitality during our visit to
Hamilton and trust this will be the beginning of a long and fruit-
ful friendship and association.

As you can well imagine things have been quite hectic since my
return after being away for two and a half months. I'm not quite
caught up yet with my patients. However, this being the month of
Ramadan (Fasting) many activities have slowed down considerably.

We're still shooting for your visit around the second week of May
and as soon as the dates are confirmed I'll give you a call.

Irma joins me in sending our kindest regards to yourself, Rosita,
her mother and the boys.

Best personal wishes.

Sincerely,

CLIVE I. MOHAMMED, D.D.S., M.S., PH.D.,
CHIEF, DENTAL SERVICES

CC: MR. JOSEPH SIRACUSA

P.O. Box 9862 - Jeddah 21159 - Saudi Arabia - Tel. Off : 669-3763 - Res : 665-3000 Ext : 2829

121

James L. Dickson Jr.

JAMES T. WALSH
MEMBER OF CONGRESS
27TH DISTRICT, NEW YORK

WASHINGTON OFFICE:
1238 LONGWORTH BUILDING
WASHINGTON, DC 20515
(202) 225-3701
(202) 225-4043 FAX

DISTRICT OFFICES:
1269 FEDERAL BUILDING
SYRACUSE, NEW YORK 13260
(315) 423-5657
(315) 423-5669 FAX

205 S. PETERBORO STREET
CANASTOTA, NEW YORK 13032
(315) 697-8414

Congress of the United States
House of Representatives
Washington, DC 20515

COMMITTEE ON AGRICULTURE
SUBCOMMITTEES:
LIVESTOCK, DAIRY, AND POULTRY
DEPARTMENT OPERATIONS, RESEARCH,
AND FOREIGN AGRICULTURE

COMMITTEE ON HOUSE ADMINISTRATION
SUBCOMMITTEES:
OFFICE SYSTEMS (RANKING)
ELECTIONS
LIBRARIES AND MEMORIALS

SELECT COMMITTEE ON CHILDREN,
YOUTH AND FAMILIES

June 13, 1990

Honorable Charles Freeman
Ambassador
American Embassy Riyadh
Collector Road M
Riyadh Diplomatic Quarter
APO New York 09038

Dear Mr. Ambassador:

I am writing on behalf of my constituent, James L. Dickson, J.L. Dickson Associates, P.O. Box 271, Hamilton, New York 13346, who will be visiting Saudi Arabia on business between June 17 and July 12, 1990.

I would appreciate it if you would extend him every possible courtesy and consideration.

Thank you for your kind attention.

Sincerely,

James T. Walsh
Member of Congress

122

J. L. DICKSON ASSOCIATES

P.O. Box 271, Hamilton, N.Y. 13346   (315) 824-1535

March 09, 1998

Ambassador Wyche Fowler, Jr.
Riyadh, Saudi Arabia

Dear Ambassador Fowler:

Thank you for your letter of February 11, 1998, to Senator D'Amato concerning my work for the king of Saudi Arabia. Following your suggestion, I will write a cover letter for the New Minister of Information for you to forward.

Please allow me to correct the impressions you have of my work and of my contacts:

    a. Almost all my work was done between me and my contact in Saudi Arabia. There were constant phone calls, many faxes and communications on a daily basis.

    b. One of my contacts in the US was with Dr. Soraya H. Al-Mashat, who was an Advisor, Information Office, for his Excellency, the Minister of Information.

Prior to this, Dr. Al-Mashat was the Director of Public Relations for the Minister of Information with an office in Jeddah.

Furthermore, in order to fully understand the importance the Saudi's placed on this project, Dr. Al-Mashat volunteered to resign her position in the Washington Embassy and dedicate her expertise to insure the success of this most important project, and as such was in contact with both me and attorney Siracusa on a regular basis over many months.

    c. The Second Secretary, Abdulrahman A. Al-Shaia, called me via a request from Minister Al-Sha'ir to continue my work here and to create a proposal for presentation to the Washington Embassy and Prince Bandar, who would then forward my work to King Fahd who initiated my being hired for this project.

    d. After the project was hand carried to Kind Fahd and the Minister of Information, I had daily, and sometimes several contacts daily, to explain, change and update my work. This was

Business Consultant

&

James L. Dickson Jr.

J. L. DICKSON ASSOCIATES

P.O. Box 271, Hamilton, N.Y. 13346   (315) 824-1535

Ambassador Wyche Fowler, Jr.
March 09, 1998
Page two

an every day activity and I spent all my time fulfilling these requests from both the Minister and King Fahd.

      e. Dr. Clive Mohammed was well known by King Fahd and the Royal Family. Not only was he their personal dentist, but he also was Chief, Dental Services, King Fahd Armed Forces Hospital in Jeddah. He was well known at your Embassy in Jeddah and also among Sheiks and many professional people that he introduced me to when I was in Saudi Arabia prior to the Gulf conflict.

I believe that I should point out that it was Kind Fahd and Minister Al-Sha'ir that contacted me and asked for me to do this project. It was also the Second Secretary that contacted me for the Minister and who kept in contact with me to arrange my work to complete the proposal and deliver same to the Embassy in Washington.

My work was not as you stated, claimed, it was long hard work on a daily basis with definitive financial arrangements stated to both me and my attorney, whose office I moved into to complete this project.

With warm regards,

JAMES L. DICKSON, JR.

bjb

Encs.

cc: Alfonso D'Amato

Business Consultant
&

124

J. L. DICKSON ASSOCIATES

P.O. Box 271, Hamilton, N.Y. 13346   (315) 824-1535

March 9, 1998

Fuad Abd al-Salam
Minister of Information
Umar, BIN AL AS Street
Riyadh, Saudi Arabia 11161

Dear Excellency:

I am enclosing herewith copies of correspondence recently sent to
Senator Alfonse D'Amato, a copy of a letter written by our Ambassador
in response, and finally a copy of a letter that I sent to Ambassador
Fowler explaining our position.

I would appreciate it if you would review this correspondence and
reply directly to me at the above address.

Your cooperation is appreciated.

Respectfully,

James L. Dickson, Jr.

bjb
Encs.

Business Consultant
&
"Marketing Specialists for the Plastic Card Industry"

125

James L. Dickson Jr.

EMBASSY OF THE
UNITED STATES OF AMERICA
RIYADH, SAUDI ARABIA

April 21, 1998

The Honorable Alfonse D'Amato
United States Senator
James M. Hanley Federal Building
100 South Clinton Street
P.O. Box 7216
Syracuse, NY 13261-7216
FAX NO.: 315-423-5185

Dear Senator D'Amato:

I have received your letter of March 27, enclosing additional correspondence from your consitituent, James Dickson.

Unfortunately, the U.S. Government cannot represent Mr. Dickson in his claim for compensation against the Saudi Government. We have gone as far as we legally can with this issue and, as I stated in my previous correspondence, it is advised that Mr. Dickson consult with legal counsel in Riyadh to determine what course of action he should take. I am again enclosing a list of local attorneys who specialize in commercial claims and who are familiar with the Saudi legal system.

Please pass this information on to your constituent. If you need additional advice or information, please don't hesitate to contact me.

Sincerely,

Wyche Fowler, Jr.
Ambassador

WF/db

126

FAX

Date   4/21/98

Number of pages including cover sheet 10

To:	From:
Marina Twomey	Debbie Burns
Office of Sen. D'Amato	Office of Amb. Fowler

Phone		Phone	011-966-1-488-3954
Fax Phone	315-423-5185	Fax Phone	011-966-1-482-2051
CC:			

REMARKS:

☐ Urgent   ☐ For your review   ☒ Reply ASAP   ☐ Please comment

Ms. Twomey,

Per our conversation yesterday, enclosed is the letter you requested as well as the attached list of attorneys in Riyadh should Mr. Dickson wish to contact them.

I hope this will satisfy your constituent (and he'll leave you alone). If you need anything else from us let me know.

Debbie

127

James L. Dickson Jr.

J. L. DICKSON ASSOCIATES

P.O. Box 271, Hamilton, N.Y. 13346   (315) 824-1535

May 13, 1998

His Royal Highness Prince Bandar
Government of Saudi Arabia
c/o Embassy
601 New Hampshire Avenue
Washington D.C. 20037

Your Royal Highness:

Though the kindness of my doctor and friend, Dr. Bashar Omarbasha, I
am writing this letter in the hope you will help me solve a very
serious problem pertaining to the work I did for His Royal Majesty
King Fahd and the Minister of Information at that time, Ali Hasson
Al'Shair, from 1990 through 1992.

Because it is not possible for me to write about thirty months of
daily work in this short correspondence, I would welcome the
opportunity to come to the Embassy and explain everything in great
detail to you, and also answer any questions you may have. I feel
very confident that you will understand how I came to be in this
predicament and hope you can help.

For your information I am including all prior correspondence which
will help explain the situation more clearly.

Thank you very much for your consideration. Hoping to hear from you
soon regarding this matter, I remain.

Respectfully Yours,

James L. Dickson, Jr.

bjb
Encs.

Business Consultant
&
"Marketing Specialists for the Plastic Card Industry"

128

SHERWOOD BOEHLERT
23D DISTRICT, NEW YORK

COMMITTEES:
SCIENCE
SUBCOMMITTEE ON BASIC RESEARCH

TRANSPORTATION AND INFRASTRUCTURE
CHAIRMAN, SUBCOMMITTEE ON
WATER RESOURCES AND ENVIRONMENT
SUBCOMMITTEE ON RAILROADS

HOUSE PERMANENT SELECT COMMITTEE
ON INTELLIGENCE

U.S. DELEGATION, NORTH ATLANTIC ASSEMBLY
CHAIRMAN, NORTHEAST AGRICULTURE CAUCUS
CHAIRMAN, MINOR LEAGUE BASEBALL CAUCUS

Congress of the United States
House of Representatives
Washington, DC 20515–3223

WASHINGTON OFFICE:
2246 RAYBURN HOUSE OFFICE BUILDING
WASHINGTON, DC 20515-3223
(202) 225-3665
Fax: (202) 225-1891
E-Mail: BOEHLERT@HR.HOUSE.GOV

CENTRAL OFFICE:
ALEXANDER PIRNIE FEDERAL BUILDING
10 BROAD STREET
UTICA, NY 13501
(315) 793-8146
Fax: (315) 798-4099

TOLL FREE: 1-800-235-2525

May 30, 1998

Mr. James L. Dickson, Jr.
President
J.L. Dickson Associates
P.O. Box 271
Hamilton, New York 13346

Dear Mr. Dickson:

My staff has informed me of the difficulties you are having contacting the appropriate parties in Saudi Arabia regarding your claim for compensation against the Saudi government. I regret that the embassy in Riyadh has not been able to provide the assistance you are seeking.

I want to let you know that I have forwarded letters on your behalf to the Department of State (DoS) in Washington and directly to the Saudi embassy in Washington. I have asked that the issues and concerns you have raised be investigated and acted upon.

I am awaiting responses and will be in touch with you as soon as I receive the requested replies. In the meantime, if you have any additional information or questions, please do not hesitate to contact me.

With warmest regards,

Sincerely,

Sherwood Boehlert
Member of Congress

SB:jd

James L. Dickson Jr.

United States Department of State

Washington, D.C. 20520

July 2, 1998

Mr. James L. Dickson, Jr.
J.L. Dickson Associates
P.O. Box 271
Hamilton, N.Y. 13346

Dear Mr. Dickson,

As we discussed, I have forwarded your letter to the Ambassador of Saudi Arabia to the United States, His Royal Highness Prince Bandar Bin Sultan. My cover letter, a copy of which is enclosed, is addressed to the Embassy's Commercial Attaché. I will inform you of any response that I receive.

I hope that this is useful to you. Please contact me if you have any questions.

Sincerely,

David B. Sullivan
Attorney-Adviser
for International Claims
and Investment Disputes

130

United States Department of State

Washington, D.C.   20520

July 2, 1998

Mr. Abdullah Al Athel
Commercial Attaché
Embassy of Saudi Arabia
601 New Hampshire Avenue, NW
Washington, D.C. 20037

Dear Mr. Al Athel,

As I explained in our telephone conversation on June
30, I am forwarding the enclosed letter to the Ambassador,
His Royal Highness Prince Bandar Bin Sultan, from Mr. James
L. Dickson, Jr., a United States citizen and the President
of J.L. Dickson Associates. Mr. Dickson states that the
Government of Saudi Arabia owes him compensation for
services rendered between 1990 and 1992.

The Department of State takes no position at this time
on the merits of Mr. Dickson's claim, but hopes that his
letter will receive careful consideration and a prompt
response. Thank you.

Sincerely,

David B. Sullivan
Attorney-Adviser
for International Claims
and Investment Disputes

131

United States Department of State

Washington, D.C. 20520

December 11, 1998

Mr. James L. Dickson, Jr.
J.L. Dickson Associates
P. O. Box 271
Hamilton, N.Y. 13346

Dear Mr. Dickson,

Enclosed is a copy of the transmittal letter to the U.S. Embassy in Riyadh, with which I enclosed your materials. I separated the materials that you provided into two packets, one for the current Minister of Information and one which we agreed should not go to the Saudi Government.

I hope that this is helpful to you. Please contact me if you have any questions.

Sincerely,

David B. Sullivan
Attorney-Adviser
for International Claims
and Investment Disputes

132

United States Department of State

Washington, D.C. 20520

November 20, 1998

John Moran
Economic Counsellor
U.S. Embassy Riyadh

Dear Mr. Moran:

Enclosed as described in a forthcoming cable are two
packets of materials concerning Mr. James Dickson. The
first packet contains correspondence and information for
forwarding to the Saudi Minister of Information. The second
packet contains additional documents for your information
only, which are not to be forwarded to the Saudi Government.
Please contact me if you have any questions. Thank you for
your assistance.

Sincerely,

David B. Sullivan
Attorney-Adviser
for International Claims
and Investment Disputes

Enclosures

James L. Dickson Jr.

United States Department of State

Washington, D.C. 20520

March 12, 1999

James L. Dickson, Jr.
J.L. Dickson Associates
P.O. Box 271
Hamilton, NY 13346

Dear Mr. Dickson,

As you requested in our phone conversation of today, enclosed is the text of a diplomatic note from Saudi Arabia dated March 1, 1999, that was received by the U.S. Embassy in Riyadh in response to the Embassy's diplomatic note of December 29, 1998. Please contact me if you have any questions.

Sincerely,

David B. Sullivan
Attorney-Adviser
for International Claims
and Investment Disputes

134

BEGIN TEXT:
WITH REFERENCE TO THE EMBASSY'S DIP NOTE NO. 1252 DATED 11/9/1419H.
IN CONNECTION WITH COMPENSATION CLAIMS MADE BY MR. JAMES DICKSON,
PRESIDENT OF DICKSON ASSOCIATES, FOR SERVICES HE ALLEGEDLY RENDERED
TO THE MINISTRY OF INFORMATION, THE MINISTRY OF FOREIGN AFFAIRS
WISHES TO ADVISE THE EMBASSY THAT THE MINISTRY OF INFORMATION HAS
RECEIVED NO CORRESPONDENCES FROM THE ABOVE MENTIONED AND THAT THE
ENTIRE CLAIM IS COMPLETELY GROUNDLESS AS FAR AS THE MINISTRY'S
RECORDS ARE CONCERNED.

END TEXT.

James L. Dickson Jr.

J. L. DICKSON ASSOCIATES

P.O. Box 271, Hamilton, N.Y. 13346   (315) 824-1535

February 23, 1999

Mr. Adel Al-Jubeir
Embassy of Saudi Arabia
601 New Hampshire Avenue NW
Washington, DC 20037

Dear Mr. Al-Jubeir:

In reference to your request that I write to his Excellency, Ali al-Shair to confirm my employment to King Fahd and Minister al-Shair, please find a journal of dates and facts that outline the major and pertinent events. This, I hope, will convince you of the legitimacy of my employment.

Your suggestion that I was "set up" by Dr. Clive Mohammed for his personal and private gain and that this was a fraud Dr. Mohammed "ran" on me is not possible when you carefully study the chronology of the facts and events.

For this to be true, his Excellency Ali al-Shair, Second Secretary Abdulrahman A. al-Shaia, Dr. Soraya Al-Mashat and life long friend Irma Mohammmed would all have had to be partners to conspire to deceive me.

Please note that this project started prior to the Gulf War and before you received twenty plus requests for a public relations project from such people as the Chancellor of Germany, America's presidents and vice presidents who contacted King Fahd, Prince Bandar and yourself.

Understand, I had no voice or control over the scope of the project and the rules of operation. Like any professional with any integrity, I followed the directions given to me and as all information was on a "need to know" basis, my activities were not a public matter.

At the time, I was not aware that this was a special project by King Fahd and Minister al-Shair and that the Embassy was not in the loop. I requested many, many times that I work through the Embassy and report to Prince Bandar and/or a subordinate of his. I very much wanted a local US presence to coordinate and give final approval to any and all special news events that I planned. If you have read my proposal, it would be clear how important this was both to me and the success we all hoped to achieve.

Business Consultant

&

"Marketing Specialists for the Plastic Card Industry"

Back to your premise that I was "used" and this was not a formal and legitimate project between me and the Kingdom of Saudi Arabia and that I never talked personally to Minister Ali al-Shair. Please allow me to show a "time line" of events that I believe proves all that I state and more:

1.   First phone call came from King Fahd's office followed by a phone call from Minister al-Shair's office, with the third call a private and personal call from Dr. Clive Mohammed from his private phone.

2.   Phone call, October 19, 1990, that the Minister had approved the project and monies would follow.

3.   November 27, 1990, phone call that requested I was to come to Saudi Arabia and have a formal meeting with King Fahd and Minister al-Shair. I faxed my agreement to a private number for delivery to Dr. Mohammed. This fax created a problem.

4.   December phone call from Dr. Mohammed for a meeting in Sarasota, Florida with my attorney as requested by Minister al-Shair.

5.   Phone call with Minister al-Shair from Dr. Mohammed's in Sarasota, Florida on January 13, 1991 when he set up my trip to meet with him and King Fahd on January 17, 1991.

6.   Twelve days later, on January 25, 1991, after my trip was delayed due to the escalation of the Gulf War, the Second Secretary, Abdulrahman A. al-Shaia called me and stated, "His Excellency, Minister Ali al-Shair had contacted the Embassy and he was directed to call me and coordinate my creating a formal proposal as soon as possible for delivery to King Fahd and Minister al-Shair."

    a.   Is it logical to assume that the Embassy and the Second Secretary were also involved in this giant scheme, and that my knowledge was needed for this group of dishonest people to make a profit? Certainly, they could have run the "scam" without me.

7.   On February 5, 1991, we had a meeting in Washington with Dr. Mohammed and Dr. Soraya Al-Mashat, a trusted employee of Minister al-Shair that was sent by him to work in the Washington Embassy and who reported to him on a regular basis.

8.   February 6, 1991, meeting in Embassy with Second Secretary and permission was given to do a survey of the Embassy and include materials and information in my proposal.

James L. Dickson Jr.

Is it really possible that so many people, two of whom were trusted employees of the Kingdom of Saudi Arabia, all planned to take advantage of me and use me for two and a half years? Could I really have meetings in your Embassy, do a survey, and use documents in my proposal? Is this possible?

It is now clear to me why I was not permitted to deliver my proposal to the Embassy. This was a special project set up to be run through the Minister of Information office and approved by the King. The Embassy was not to be involved. All my activities were to be coordinated directly from the Minister of Information office. Dr. Soraya Al-Mashat would be my only local Saudi contact.

Thank you for your assistance. I wish this had been a more open project, but now I understand the secrecy. If you need more information, I am at your service.

Respectfully,

JAMES L. DICKSON, JR.

JLD/drk

J. L. DICKSON ASSOCIATES

P.O. Box 271, Hamilton, N.Y. 13346   (315) 824-1535

April 26, 1999

Mr. Adel Al-Jubeir
Embassy of Saudi Arabia
601 New Hampshire Avenue, NW
Washington DC 20037

Dear Mr. Al-Jubeir:

On December 29, 1998 the U.S. Embassy in Riyadh, Saudi Arabia, sent a diplomatic note to your Ministry of Foreign Affairs office to discover what correspondence the Ministry of Information office had relating to my public relations project. The March 1, 1991 reply stated that "the Ministry of Information has received no correspondences from the above mentioned (J.L. Dickson) and that the entire claim is completely groundless as far as the Ministry's records are concerned".

This brings the question of what happened to the following correspondence, each of which was sent to the Minister of Information office in Riyadh, Saudi Arabia.

A. January 22, 1998 letter from me sent directly to Minister Al-Shair.

B. March 9, 1998 letter from me sent by the U.S. State Department. Letter addressed to Minister Al-Salam.

C. May 13, 1998 letter from me addressed to His Royal Highness Prince Bandar that was personally delivered to Prince Bandar's Secretary. You stated in our conversation that you had reviewed all the correspondence contained in this delivery and had forwarded it to the Minister of Information office and they had replied to you that there were no records of previous correspondences. This answer being given to you months prior to the U.S. State Department's diplomatic note being sent in December 1998.

D. November 20, 1998 letter from David Sullivan (U.S. Department of State) to John Moran, Economic Counsellor, U.S. Embassy in Riyadh.

Business Consultant
&
"Marketing Specialists for the Plastic Card Industry"

139

It is not surprising that the Ministry of Information office cannot locate all the work I did for that office in 1990, 1991, and 1992 when correspondence sent by me in January, 1998, the U.S. State Department correspondence sent in the spring of 1998, and the correspondence sent by you from the Washington Embassy in the summer of 1998 is also lost.

If I am to be treated fairly and compensated properly for work I did, then I will need your help. I cannot make lost records appear, but you can verify my claims by checking:

1. Phone records from the embassy to me.

2. Phone records from Saudi Arabia facilities in Saudi Arabia to me.

3. Asking why Dr. Soraya Al-Mashat, a trusted employee of Minister Al-Shair, who was in constant contact with him and Dr. Mohammed, why she verified all of the information given to me from Dr. Mohammed and wanted so much to be a part of this project that she sent me her vita.

   Dr. Al-Mashat explained to me why it took so long for a project to be approved and that it would take at least three months for the budget to be approved.

   I doubt she would show this interest if not assured by Minister Al-Shair that this was his project approved by King Fahd.

4. Second Secretary, Abdulrahman A. Al-Shaia and the phone calls we had, plus my visit to deliver the proposal plus his approval for me to do a survey of the embassy to see if it could help this most important project of King Fahd.

Please help! Thank you!

Sincerely,

James L. Dickson, Jr.

SHERWOOD BOEHLERT
23D District, New York

COMMITTEES:
SCIENCE
SUBCOMMITTEE ON BASIC RESEARCH

TRANSPORTATION AND INFRASTRUCTURE
CHAIRMAN, SUBCOMMITTEE ON
WATER RESOURCES AND ENVIRONMENT
SUBCOMMITTEE ON RAILROADS

HOUSE PERMANENT SELECT COMMITTEE
ON INTELLIGENCE

U.S. DELEGATION, NORTH ATLANTIC ASSEMBLY
CHAIRMAN, NORTHEAST AGRICULTURE CAUCUS
CHAIRMAN, MINOR LEAGUE BASEBALL CAUCUS

Congress of the United States
House of Representatives
Washington, DC 20515–3223
May 20, 1999

WASHINGTON OFFICE:
2246 RAYBURN HOUSE OFFICE BUILDING
WASHINGTON, DC 20515–3223
(202) 225–3665
Fax: (202) 225–1891
E-Mail: rep.boehlert@mail.house.gov

CENTRAL OFFICE:
ALEXANDER PIRNIE FEDERAL BUILDING
10 BROAD STREET
UTICA, NY 13501
(315) 793–8146
Fax: (315) 798–4099

TOLL FREE: 1–800–236–2526

Mr. James L. Dickson, Jr.
P.O. Box 271
Hamilton, New York 13346

Dear Mr. Dickson:

I'm writing to confirm receipt of the information you sent to my office and to let you know that I've forwarded copies to Mr. Sullivan and Ms. Pratt for follow through. I regret that efforts to date to elicit a response from the Saudi government have been unsuccessful.

I've expressed my dissatisfaction to both parties that they have been unable to bring the appropriate pressure to bear with regard to your request for assistance in processing your claim.

As soon as I receive a response, I'll be in touch. In the meantime, if you have any additional information or further questions or concerns, do not hesitate to contact me.

With warmest regards,

Sincerely,

Sherwood Boehlert
Member of Congress

SB:jd

141

James L. Dickson Jr.

July 31, 1999

Mrs. Hilary Rodham Clinton
1600 Pennsylvania Avenue
Washington, D.C. 20500

Dear Hilary:

I need your help! If you were presently a New York Senator I
would be the first person at your congressional office
explaining to one of your staff, in great detail, the very
serious problem I have had as a consultant for two and one-
half years for King Fahd and Minister Ali al Shair of the
Kingdom of Saudi Arabia. (Minister al Shair left office
August 1995.)

One well placed phone call by you would get the results that
over two years of efforts by past and present members of
Congress and the State Department could not and have not been
able to do. Unfortunately, their level of contact is not on a
high enough level to even obtain a response to my
correspondence. The Saudis simply do not reply because they
know our system at that level does not require any action to
be taken.

Their reply to a diplomatic note sent by the State Department
was that they had received NO correspondences related to J.L.
Dickson. This was after the State Department had sent
documents from me on three occasions and I had sent the
documents on six occasions. Again they understand that by
ignoring and or denying my claim the problem to them would go
away. That the American political system isn't set up to do
more for the average American citizen than a letter or phone
call, and the courtesy of a reply is not necessary if you want
the problem to go away.

Yes, I fully understand that for me to ask for an hour of the
First Lady's time is not normally done. But this letter
appeals to that special person running to become a Senator of
New York, and she has abilities that other members of Congress
do not have. The ability to actually solve problems and not
to just talk about solutions.

142

One hour of your time and one phone call would make a huge difference in the lives of the entire Dickson family. It would correct a wrong and send a message that each and every American is important, not just our VIP's. Isn't it time that the average American receives the help from government that is now reserved for the few?

Will you help?

Sincerely,

James L. Dickson, Jr.

James L. Dickson Jr.

SHERWOOD BOEHLERT
23D DISTRICT, NEW YORK

COMMITTEES:
SCIENCE
SUBCOMMITTEE ON BASIC RESEARCH

TRANSPORTATION AND INFRASTRUCTURE
CHAIRMAN, SUBCOMMITTEE ON
WATER RESOURCES AND ENVIRONMENT
SUBCOMMITTEE ON RAILROADS

HOUSE PERMANENT SELECT COMMITTEE
ON INTELLIGENCE

U.S. DELEGATION, NORTH ATLANTIC ASSEMBLY
CHAIRMAN, NORTHEAST AGRICULTURE CAUCUS
CHAIRMAN, MINOR LEAGUE BASEBALL CAUCUS

Congress of the United States
House of Representatives
Washington, DC 20515–3223

WASHINGTON OFFICE:
2248 RAYBURN HOUSE OFFICE BUILDING
WASHINGTON, DC 20515–3223
(202) 225–3665
Fax: (202) 225–1891
E-Mail: rep.boehlert@mail.house.gov

CENTRAL OFFICE:
ALEXANDER PIRNIE FEDERAL BUILDING
10 BROAD STREET
UTICA, NY 13501
(315) 793–8146
Fax: (315) 798–4099

TOLL FREE: 1–800–235–2525

August 6, 1999

Mr. James L. Dickson, Jr.
P.O. Box 271
Hamilton, New York 13346

Dear Mr. Dickson:

I appreciate the continued opportunity to try to be of assistance to you.

I have again contacted both Ginny Pratt and David Sullivan at the Department of State on your behalf. They assure me that they are continuing to work on your case in an effort to get your paperwork directly to Adel Al-Jubeir in Saudi Arabia. They are also aware that I am very interested in seeing that your case receives top priority. As soon as I receive further responses, I will be sure to let you know.

In the meantime, if you have any further questions or wish to share additional information, please do no hesitate to contact me at my Utica District Office.

With warmest regards,

Sincerely,

Sherwood Boehlert
Member of Congress

SB:ut1

144

SHERWOOD BOEHLERT
23D DISTRICT, NEW YORK

COMMITTEES:
SCIENCE
SUBCOMMITTEE ON BASIC RESEARCH

TRANSPORTATION AND INFRASTRUCTURE
CHAIRMAN, SUBCOMMITTEE ON
WATER RESOURCES AND ENVIRONMENT
SUBCOMMITTEE ON RAILROADS

HOUSE PERMANENT SELECT COMMITTEE
ON INTELLIGENCE

U.S. DELEGATION, NORTH ATLANTIC ASSEMBLY
CHAIRMAN, NORTHEAST AGRICULTURE CAUCUS
CHAIRMAN, MINOR LEAGUE BASEBALL CAUCUS

Congress of the United States
House of Representatives
Washington, DC 20515–3223

WASHINGTON OFFICE:
2246 RAYBURN HOUSE OFFICE BUILDING
WASHINGTON, DC 20515-3223
(202) 225-3665
Fax: (202) 225-1891
E-Mail: rep.boehlert@mail.house.gov

CENTRAL OFFICE:
ALEXANDER PIRNIE FEDERAL BUILDING
10 BROAD STREET
UTICA, NY 13501
(315) 793-8146
Fax: (315) 798-4099

TOLL FREE: 1-800-235-2525

September 16, 1999

Mr. James L. Dickson, Jr.
P.O. Box 271
Hamilton, New York 13346

Dear Mr. Dickson:

Enclosed is the most recent correspondence I have received from the Department of State (DoS). I regret that it could not have been more substantive given the amount of time that you have been trying to get a response from the Saudi government.

I have also spoken directly with Mr. Sullivan who is aware of my interest in bringing this matter to an acceptable conclusion and has given me his assurances that DoS will monitor the inquiry until you receive a reply.

As soon as I have any further information, I will be in touch.

With warmest regards,

Sincerely,

Sherwood Boehlert
Member of Congress

SB:jd
Enclosure

James L. Dickson Jr.

United States Department of State

Washington, D.C. 20520

AUG 3 1 1999

Dear Mr. Boehlert:

This is in response to your letter of May 20 addressed to Mr. David Sullivan, Attorney-Adviser in the Office of the Legal Adviser, concerning the claims against the government of Saudi Arabia of your constituent Mr. James L. Dickson, Jr.

The State Department understands and shares Mr. Dickson's frustration with the lack of response he has received from the Saudi government. Both the Department and the U.S. Embassy in Riyadh will continue to assist Mr. Dickson, as appropriate, in his efforts to achieve a satisfactory resolution of his dispute.

In response to your request, the Department will send to Mr. Adel Al-Jubeir, First Secretary at the Embassy of Saudi Arabia, copies of Mr. Dickson's correspondence of February 23, April 21 and April 26. The Department will also express concern that Mr. Dickson has received no acknowledgment or response, ask about the status of Mr. Dickson's inquiries, and request a response at Mr. Al-Jubeir's earliest convenience. As you requested, Department officials will monitor this matter until Mr. Dickson has received a reply.

We trust that this information will prove helpful in responding to your constituent. Please do not hesitate to contact us if you believe that we may be of further assistance in this, or any other, matter.

Sincerely,

Barbara Larkin
Assistant Secretary
Legislative Affairs

Enclosure:
        Correspondence returned.

The Honorable
        Sherwood Boehlert,
        House of Representatives.

SHERWOOD BOEHLERT
23D DISTRICT, NEW YORK

COMMITTEES:
SCIENCE
SUBCOMMITTEE ON BASIC RESEARCH

TRANSPORTATION AND INFRASTRUCTURE
CHAIRMAN, SUBCOMMITTEE ON
WATER RESOURCES AND ENVIRONMENT
SUBCOMMITTEE ON RAILROADS

HOUSE PERMANENT SELECT COMMITTEE
ON INTELLIGENCE

U.S. DELEGATION, NORTH ATLANTIC ASSEMBLY
CHAIRMAN, NORTHEAST AGRICULTURE CAUCUS
CHAIRMAN, MINOR LEAGUE BASEBALL CAUCUS

Congress of the United States
House of Representatives
Washington, DC 20515–3223

WASHINGTON OFFICE:
2246 RAYBURN HOUSE OFFICE BUILDING
WASHINGTON, DC 20515–3223
(202) 225–3665
Fax: (202) 225–1891
E-Mail: rep.boehlert@mail.house.gov

CENTRAL OFFICE:
ALEXANDER PIRNIE FEDERAL BUILDING
10 BROAD STREET
UTICA, NY 13501
(315) 793–8146
Fax: (315) 798–4099

TOLL FREE: 1–800–235–2525

January 7, 2000

Mr. James L. Dickson, Jr.
P.O. Box 271
Hamilton, New York 13346

Dear Mr. Dickson:

I am writing to confirm receipt of the copy of the letter you sent to Mr. Al-Jubeir regarding your ongoing efforts to collect the monies owed you for the work you did for the Saudi government. It is unfortunate that the matter is still unresolved. I know that you are frustrated and disappointed that actions to date have not brought about an acceptable resolution.

I will continue to try to assist you in establishing contact with Saudi officials in a position to address your claim. Enclosed is a copy of correspondence I have directed to Prince Bandar in Washington on your behalf. I am hopeful that my request for his assistance will produce some positive results.

As soon as I receive a response, I will be in touch. In the meantime, if you have any additional information or further concerns, do not hesitate to contact me.

With warmest regards,

Sincerely,

Sherwood Boehlert
Member of Congress

SB:jd
Enclosure

147

James L. Dickson Jr.

SHERWOOD BOEHLERT
23D DISTRICT, NEW YORK

COMMITTEES:
SCIENCE
SUBCOMMITTEE ON BASIC RESEARCH

TRANSPORTATION AND INFRASTRUCTURE
CHAIRMAN, SUBCOMMITTEE ON
WATER RESOURCES AND ENVIRONMENT
SUBCOMMITTEE ON RAILROADS

HOUSE PERMANENT SELECT COMMITTEE
ON INTELLIGENCE

U.S. DELEGATION, NORTH ATLANTIC ASSEMBLY
CHAIRMAN, NORTHEAST AGRICULTURE CAUCUS
CHAIRMAN, MINOR LEAGUE BASEBALL CAUCUS

Congress of the United States
House of Representatives
Washington, DC 20515–3223

WASHINGTON OFFICE:
2246 RAYBURN HOUSE OFFICE BUILDING
WASHINGTON, DC 20515–3223
(202) 225-3665
Fax: (202) 225-1891
E-Mail: rep.boehlert@mail.house.gov

CENTRAL OFFICE:
ALEXANDER PIRNIE FEDERAL BUILDING
10 BROAD STREET
UTICA, NY 13501
(315) 793-8146
Fax: (315) 796-4099

TOLL FREE: 1-800-235-2525

January 7, 2000

H.R.H. Prince Bandar Bin Sultan
Embassy Of Saudi Arabia
601 New Hampshire Ave NW
Washington, D.C. 20037

Dear Excellency:

Enclosed is a copy of a letter recently sent to Adel al-Jubier by my constituent, James L. Dickson, Jr., President, J.L. Dickson Associates, regarding his efforts to file a claim for compensation with the Saudi Arabian government.

I have previously corresponded with you on behalf of Mr Dickson who seeks reimbursement for a public relations project he created at the request of King Fahd and Minister Ali al Shair. My previous letter to you (copy enclosed) was never acknowledged. Additionally, the Department of State (DoS) has attempted to assist Mr. Dickson in establishing contact with Saudi officials in a position to address his claim. To date, all actions taken to resolve this matter have proven unsuccessful. All inquires have gone unanswered.

I remain confident that with your assistance and direction, Mr. Dickson will be afforded the opportunity to present his case for consideration and appropriate compensation. I am enclosing background information which I believe will be helpful in establishing the legitimacy of his request.

I appreciate your attention to this issue and ask that you inform me of what steps Mr. Dickson needs to take from this point to process his claim. Please direct your response to my District Office, Alexander Pirnie Federal Building, Room 200, 10 Broad Street, Utica, New York, 13501-1270.

Thank you for your interest and attention. I look forward to hearing from you.

With warmest regards,

Sincerely,

Sherwood Boehlert
Member of Congress

SB:jd
Enclosure

SHERWOOD BOEHLERT
23o District, New York

COMMITTEES:
SCIENCE
SUBCOMMITTEE ON BASIC RESEARCH

TRANSPORTATION AND INFRASTRUCTURE
CHAIRMAN, SUBCOMMITTEE ON
WATER RESOURCES AND ENVIRONMENT
SUBCOMMITTEE ON RAILROADS

HOUSE PERMANENT SELECT COMMITTEE
ON INTELLIGENCE

U.S. DELEGATION, NORTH ATLANTIC ASSEMBLY
CHAIRMAN, NORTHEAST AGRICULTURE CAUCUS
CHAIRMAN, MINOR LEAGUE BASEBALL CAUCUS

Congress of the United States
House of Representatives
Washington, DC 20515–3223
February 14, 2000

WASHINGTON OFFICE:
2246 RAYBURN HOUSE OFFICE BUILDING
WASHINGTON, DC 20515–3223
(202) 225-3665
Fax: (202) 225-1891
E-Mail: rep.boehlert@mail.house.gov

CENTRAL OFFICE:
ALEXANDER PIRNIE FEDERAL BUILDING
10 BROAD STREET
UTICA, NY 13501
(315) 793-8146
Fax: (315) 798-4099

TOLL FREE: 1-800-235-2525

The Honorable Madeleine K. Albright
Secretary
U.S. Department of State
2201 C Street, N.W.
Washington, D.C. 20520

Dear Madame Secretary:

I am enclosing a copy of a letter addressed to Adel al-Jubier, Minister of Information, Embassy of Saudi Arabia, by my constituent, James L. Dickson, Jr., J.L. Dickson Associates, regarding his efforts to file a claim for compensation with the Saudi Arabian government. On January 7, 2000, I forwarded Mr. Dickson's letter to Prince Bandar Bin Sultan along with a personal request that he be afforded the opportunity to present his case for consideration and appropriate compensation. To date, there has been no response from the embassy.

Since May 1998, I have attempted to assist Mr. Dickson in his efforts to contact the Saudi government. I previously wrote directly to the embassy and have been in contact with the Department of State's (DoS) Office of the Legal Advisor and Saudi Arabian desk officer. While your staff has been responsive and has followed through on Mr. Dickson's behalf, no progress has been made to date in eliciting any type of direction from Saudi officials on how to proceed. It appears that written inquires to the embassy are easily ignored.

Mr. Dickson is understandably frustrated and angry that his government and elected representatives are unable to establish contact for him with the embassy. He has asked that I bring this matter to your attention. What further steps can be taken at this point to assist Mr. Dickson?

I am enclosing background information which Mr. Dickson has provided outlining his situation and he is available to respond to any questions you may have regarding the work he did, contacts, etc..

Please reply to my District Office, Alexander Pirnie Federal Building, Room 200, 10 Broad Street, Utica, New York, 13501-1270.

Thank you for your attention and cooperation. I look forward to hearing from you.

With warmest regards,

Sincerely,

Sherwood Boehlert
Member of Congress

SB:jd
Enclosure

James L. Dickson Jr.

SHERWOOD BOEHLERT
23D DISTRICT, NEW YORK

COMMITTEES:
SCIENCE
SUBCOMMITTEE ON BASIC RESEARCH

TRANSPORTATION AND INFRASTRUCTURE
CHAIRMAN, SUBCOMMITTEE ON
WATER RESOURCES AND ENVIRONMENT
SUBCOMMITTEE ON RAILROADS

HOUSE PERMANENT SELECT COMMITTEE
ON INTELLIGENCE

U.S. DELEGATION, NORTH ATLANTIC ASSEMBLY
CHAIRMAN, NORTHEAST AGRICULTURE CAUCUS
CHAIRMAN, MINOR LEAGUE BASEBALL CAUCUS

Congress of the United States
House of Representatives
Washington, DC 20515—3223

WASHINGTON OFFICE:
2246 RAYBURN HOUSE OFFICE BUILDING
WASHINGTON, DC 20515—3223
(202) 225-3665
Fax: (202) 225-1891
E-Mail: rep.boehlert@mail.house.gov

CENTRAL OFFICE:
ALEXANDER PIRNIE FEDERAL BUILDING
10 BROAD STREET
UTICA, NY 13501
(315) 793-8146
Fax: (315) 798-4099

TOLL FREE: 1-800-235-2525

March 22, 2000

The Honorable Madeleine K. Albright
Secretary
U.S. Department Of State
2201 C Street, N.W.
Washington, D.C. 20520

Dear Madame Secretary:

On February 24, 2000, I contacted you on behalf of my constituent, James L. Dickson, Jr., J.L. Dickson Associates, regarding his efforts to file a claim for compensation with the Saudi Arabian government.

To date, I have not received a reply. I am enclosing a copy of my initial correspondence for reference.

Mr. Dickson is anxious to resolve this matter. I would appreciate your immediate attention to his request for assistance. Please direct your response to my District Office, Alexander Pirnie Federal Building, Room 200, 10 Broad Street, Utica, New York, 13501.

Thank you for your immediate attention. I look forward to hearing from you.

With warmest regards,

Sincerely,

Sherwood Boehlert
Member of Congress

SB:jd
Enclosure

150

SHERWOOD BOEHLERT
23rd District, New York

COMMITTEES:
SCIENCE
SUBCOMMITTEE ON BASIC RESEARCH

TRANSPORTATION AND INFRASTRUCTURE
CHAIRMAN, SUBCOMMITTEE ON
WATER RESOURCES AND ENVIRONMENT
SUBCOMMITTEE ON RAILROADS

HOUSE PERMANENT SELECT COMMITTEE
ON INTELLIGENCE

U.S. DELEGATION, NORTH ATLANTIC ASSEMBLY
CHAIRMAN, NORTHEAST AGRICULTURE CAUCUS
CHAIRMAN, MINOR LEAGUE BASEBALL CAUCUS

Congress of the United States
House of Representatives
Washington, DC 20515-3223

WASHINGTON OFFICE:
2246 RAYBURN HOUSE OFFICE BUILDING
WASHINGTON, DC 20515-3223
(202) 225-3665
Fax: (202) 225-1891
E-Mail: rep.boehlert@mail.house.gov

CENTRAL OFFICE:
ALEXANDER PIRNIE FEDERAL BUILDING
10 BROAD STREET
UTICA, NY 13501
(315) 793-8146
Fax: (315) 798-4099

TOLL FREE: 1-800-235-2525

April 3, 2000

H.R.H. Prince Bandar Bin Sultan
Embassy Of Saudi Arabia
601 New Hampshire Ave NW
Washington, D.C. 20037

Dear Excellency:

On January 7, 2000, I contacted you on behalf of my constituent, James L. Dickson, President, J.L. Dickson Associates, regarding his efforts to file a claim for compensation with the Saudi Arabian government.

To date, I have not received a reply. I am enclosing a copy of my initial correspondence for your reference.

Mr. Dickson is anxious to resolve this matter. I would appreciate your immediate attention to his request for assistance. Please direct your reply to my District Office, Alexander Pirnie Federal Building, Room 200, 10 Broad Street, Utica, New York, 13501.

Thank you for your immediate attention. I look forward to hearing from you.

With warmest regards,

Sincerely,

Sherwood Boehlert
Member of Congress

SB:jd
Enclosure

James L. Dickson Jr.

وزارة الخارجية
سفارة المملكة العربية السعودية واشنطن

ROYAL EMBASSY OF SAUDI ARABIA
WASHINGTON, D.C. 20037

April 12, 2000

Mr. J. L. Dickson
P.O. Box 271
Hamilton, N.Y. 13346

Dear Mr. Dickson:

I am responding to your letter dated December 7, 1999.

When I spoke with you about this matter, I asked you to forward any evidence of a contract between you and any entity of the Saudi government for the Embassy's review. I stated clearly what was required, and informed you that verbal agreements between you and Dr. Clive Mohamed, who is not an employee of this Embassy, are not the responsibility of this Embassy. I also stated that conversations between you and Embassy employees with no authority to commit the Saudi government, and who have long since left the Embassy, would not suffice. I believed that you would submit this evidence, but you have not done so. All I received was a list of events which you purport took place, without any documentation indicating the existence of any agreement between you and any entity of the Saudi government.

Several years ago, when you first contacted this Embassy, your claim was forwarded to the appropriate authorities in the Kingdom. At the time, the Minister of Information indicated that he knew of no agreement with you. I believe the American Embassy in Riyadh received the same response when it requested information on your behalf. I explained this to you in our telephone conversation.

May I suggest that you contact Dr. Clive Mohamed, who you claim was responsible for asking you to initiate your efforts and settle this matter directly with him. The Embassy was not a party to any agreements you may or may not have made with him, and, consequently, is not in any position to determine the validity of your claim.

Sincerely,

Adel A. Al-Jubeir
First Secretary

152

SHERWOOD BOEHLERT
23D DISTRICT, NEW YORK

COMMITTEES:
SCIENCE
SUBCOMMITTEE ON BASIC RESEARCH

TRANSPORTATION AND INFRASTRUCTURE
CHAIRMAN, SUBCOMMITTEE ON
WATER RESOURCES AND ENVIRONMENT
SUBCOMMITTEE ON RAILROADS

HOUSE PERMANENT SELECT COMMITTEE
ON INTELLIGENCE

U.S. DELEGATION, NORTH ATLANTIC ASSEMBLY
CHAIRMAN, NORTHEAST AGRICULTURE CAUCUS
CHAIRMAN, MINOR LEAGUE BASEBALL CAUCUS

Congress of the United States
House of Representatives
Washington, DC 20515–3223

WASHINGTON OFFICE:
2246 RAYBURN HOUSE OFFICE BUILDING
WASHINGTON, DC 20515–3223
(202) 225-3665
Fax: (202) 225-1891
E-Mail: rep.boehlert@mail.house.gov

CENTRAL OFFICE:
ALEXANDER PIRNIE FEDERAL BUILDING
10 BROAD STREET
UTICA, NY 13501
(315) 793-8146
Fax: (315) 798-4099

TOLL FREE: 1–800–235–2525

May 2, 2000

Mr. James L. Dickson, Jr.
P.O. Box 271
Hamilton, New York 13346

Dear Mr. Dickson:

I'm enclosing a copy of the response I've received from Ambassador Badar bin Sultan bin Abdulaziz in reply to my most recent inquiry on your behalf. It's my understanding that First Secretary Adel A. Al-Jubeir has also corresponded directly with you stating the embassy's position with regard to your compensation claim.

I'm awaiting feedback from the Department of State (DoS) and will be in touch when I have any further information to pass along.

With warmest regards,

Sincerely,

Sherwood Boehlert
Member of Congress

SB:jd
Enclosure

153

James L. Dickson Jr.

APR 2 0 2000

سفارة المملكة العربية السعودية
في واشنطن

ROYAL EMBASSY OF SAUDI ARABIA
601 NEW HAMPSHIRE AVENUE, N. W.
WASHINGTON, D. C. 20037

OFFICE OF
THE AMBASSADOR

April 13, 2000

The Honorable Sherwood Boehlert
Member of Congress
Alexander Pirnie Federal Building
Room 200
10 Broad Street
Utica, New York 13501-1270

Dear Congressman Boehlert:

I am responding to your letter dated January 7, 2000 regarding the claim of your constituent, Mr. James L. Dickson.

I have asked my assistant, Mr. Adel Al-Jubeir to respond directly to Mr. Dickson, and I am enclosing a copy of his response with this letter, which I believe is self-explanatory. I am also enclosing a copy of the text of the diplomatic note, which your embassy in Riyadh received from the Saudi Arabian Ministry of Foreign Affairs on this matter and which was included in the attachments you sent me in your above-referenced letter.

With best personal regards,

Sincerely,

Bandar bin Sultan bin Abdulaziz
Ambassador

BbSbA/sc

154

SHERWOOD BOEHLERT
23D DISTRICT, NEW YORK

COMMITTEES:
SCIENCE
SUBCOMMITTEE ON BASIC RESEARCH

TRANSPORTATION AND INFRASTRUCTURE
CHAIRMAN, SUBCOMMITTEE ON
WATER RESOURCES AND ENVIRONMENT
SUBCOMMITTEE ON RAILROADS

HOUSE PERMANENT SELECT COMMITTEE
ON INTELLIGENCE

U.S. DELEGATION, NORTH ATLANTIC ASSEMBLY
CHAIRMAN, NORTHEAST AGRICULTURE CAUCUS
CHAIRMAN, MINOR LEAGUE BASEBALL CAUCUS

Congress of the United States
House of Representatives
Washington, DC 20515–3223

WASHINGTON OFFICE:
2246 RAYBURN HOUSE OFFICE BUILDING
WASHINGTON, DC 20615–3223
(202) 225–3665
Fax: (202) 225–1891
E-Mail: rep.boehlert@mail.house.gov

CENTRAL OFFICE:
ALEXANDER PIRNIE FEDERAL BUILDING
10 BROAD STREET
UTICA, NY 13501
(315) 793–8146
Fax: (315) 798–4099

TOLL FREE: 1–800–235–2525

June 12, 2000

Mr. James L. Dickson, Jr.
P.O. Box 271
Hamilton, New York 13346

Dear Mr. Dickson:

As you will learn from reading the enclosed letter to Assistant Secretary of State Barbara Larkin, I'm doing my best to get attention for your case at a high level within our government.

Your case has been dragging on for several years and previously involved Senator D'Amato. The problem then, as it may still be, was a lack of hard evidence (signed contracts, correspondence, etc.) to move your claim.

I'm willing to give it another try, but you must understand at the outset that this is by no means a simple matter.

I'll be in touch when I have a response to my latest inquiry.

Sincerely,

Sherwood Boehlert
Member of Congress

155

James L. Dickson Jr.

SHERWOOD BOEHLERT
23d District, New York

COMMITTEES:
SCIENCE
SUBCOMMITTEE ON BASIC RESEARCH
—
TRANSPORTATION AND INFRASTRUCTURE
CHAIRMAN, SUBCOMMITTEE ON
WATER RESOURCES AND ENVIRONMENT
SUBCOMMITTEE ON RAILROADS
—
HOUSE PERMANENT SELECT COMMITTEE
ON INTELLIGENCE
—
U.S. DELEGATION, NORTH ATLANTIC ASSEMBLY
CHAIRMAN, NORTHEAST AGRICULTURE CAUCUS
CHAIRMAN, MINOR LEAGUE BASEBALL CAUCUS

Congress of the United States
House of Representatives
Washington, DC 20515–3223

WASHINGTON OFFICE:
2246 RAYBURN HOUSE OFFICE BUILDING
WASHINGTON, DC 20515–3223
(202) 225-3665
Fax: (202) 225-1891
E-Mail: rep.boehlert@mail.house.gov

CENTRAL OFFICE:
ALEXANDER PIRNIE FEDERAL BUILDING
10 BROAD STREET
UTICA, NY 13501
(315) 793-8146
Fax: (315) 798-4099

TOLL FREE: 1-800-235-2525

June 12, 2000

The Honorable Barbara Larkin
Assistant Secretary
Bureau of Legislative Affairs
Department of State
2201 C Street
Washington, D.C. 20520

Dear Ms. Barbara:

Following receipt of your May 24, 2000 letter pertaining to the case of my constituent, James L. Dickson, Jr., President of J. L. Dickson Associates, in his dispute with the government of Saudi Arabia, I had a lengthy personal meeting with Mr. Dickson in my district office.

I came away from that meeting convinced that this case demands further consideration and consequently am formally requesting your assistance in setting up a meeting with the appropriate person(s) within the State Department to hear out Mr. Dickson. (David Sullivan?).

The lengthy presentation from Mr. Dickson to me led me to the conclusion that there are a great many coincidences and much circumstantial evidence to prompt a reasonable assumption that there is legitimacy to Mr. Dickson's claim that he was given the go-ahead to implement a plan to benefit the government of Saudi Arabia and that he was not compensated for the work. Who precisely gave the O.K. to do the work and what the stipulations and expectations were is an open question.

The bottom line is that I feel that Mr. Dickson is not letting his imagination run wild and that he is deserving further consideration of his case by the appropriate official(s) of our government.

I am anxious for your reaction.

Sincerely,

Sherwood Boehlert
Member of Congress

156

JUN 05 2000

United States Department of State

Washington, D.C. 20520

MAY 2 4 2000

Dear Mr. Boehlert,

   Thank you for your letters of February 24 and March 22 concerning your constituent James L. Dickson, Jr., President of J. L. Dickson Associates. We apologize for the delay in responding. Your correspondence concerned the lack of a response from the Embassy of Saudi Arabia to several letters about Mr. Dickson's claims for compensation.

   Following Mr. Dickson's letter to the Saudi Embassy of February 23, 1999, and his several subsequent letters, the Department contacted Embassy officials several times, both orally and in writing, expressing concern about this matter and about the Embassy's lack of a response. Your letter to the Embassy of January 7 expressed similar concerns.

   The Embassy recently provided to us copies of letters from Ambassador HRH Prince Baudar bin Sultan to you, of April 13, and from First Secretary Adel A. Al-Jubeir to Mr. Dickson, of April 12. Copies of this correspondence are enclosed. We share Mr. Dickson's disappointment with the Saudi's slow response to his, your and the Department's many inquiries.

   Mr. Al-Jubeir wrote to Mr. Dickson that he found no documentation "indicating the existence of any agreement between you and any entity of the Saudi government." Mr. Dickson has previously stated that he will not pursue his claim under the Saudi legal system, and that he hoped the Embassy would recognize the validity of his claim. In these circumstances, the Department is unable to pursue this matter any further with the

The Honorable
    Sherwood Boehlert,
        House of Representatives.

157

James L. Dickson Jr.

Saudi government.   We regret that our reply cannot be more
encouraging.

                    Sincerely,

                    Barbara Larkin
                    Assistant Secretary
                    Legislative Affairs

Enclosures:
    1. Correspondence returned.
    2. Correspondence from Embassy of Saudi Arabia.

June 20, 2000

Mr. James L. Dickson, Jr.
J. L. Dickson Associates
P.O. Box 271
Hamilton, N.Y. 13346

Dear Mr. Dickson:

I am responding to your letter dated May 1, 2000.

I do not believe that any of the facts in the matter have changed. You state that you performed work for the former Minister of Information, but you do not provide any proof thereof. The fact that you had contact with officials at this Embassy is not sufficient proof of an agreement to perform work. Finally, the person you allegedly worked for (the former Minister of Information) does not have any knowledge of any such agreement. He informed the Embassy of this when this matter first came up, and my government informed the American Embassy in the Kingdom of the same when officially asked about it last year.

For the record, I would like to correct an inaccuracy in your letter. In your letter you state that "you [meaning I] agreed the work was done ..". This is absolutely not correct. I never said such a thing. In fact, I never heard of you until you started writing and calling me.

I hope the above clarifies matters, as I hope that you will understand that I cannot continue in a permanent dialogue with you about this issue.

Sincerely,

Adel A. Al-Jubeir
First Secretary

159

James L. Dickson Jr.

July 9, 2000

His Royal Highness Prince Bandar bin Sultan
Royal Embassy of Saudi Arabia
601 New Hampshire Avenue, N.W.
Washington D.C. 20037

Your Royal Highness:

Please find enclosed a copy of the letter I sent to your assistant, First Secretary Adel Al-Jubeir, dated May 1, 2000 in response to his letter of April 12, 2000. The First secretary made the following points in his letter:

1. He wanted me to forward to him a signed contract between either King Fahad or Minister Ali Al-Shair and myself.
2. That the conversation between me and Second Secretary Abdulrahman Al-Shaia and Dr. Soraya Al-Mashat did not commit the Embassy.
3. To contact Dr. Clive Mohammed and settle this matter directly with him.
4. That several years ago he contacted the Minister of Information and he did not know J.L. Dickson and that the U.S. State Department had the same response from their request.

My letter of May 1, 2000 covers each of these points, as follows:

1. He did not request me to forward a signed contract because he knew there was no written contract. We had discussed this at great length. He did ask me to write Minister Al-Shair to refresh his memory and send the correspondence to him for mailing by the Embassy to the Minister.

2. The Second Secretary called me and claimed he had the authority, plus he was acting for Minister Al-Shair, who had called the Embassy and requested that I finish the proposal as soon as possible and deliver the proposal to the Second Secretary at the Embassy for immediate delivery to him as King Fahd was waiting on it.

3. Dr. Al-Mashat informed me that Dr. Mohammed had committed suicide.

In your letter to Congressman Sherwood Boehlert, dated April 13, 2000 you made the point of sending him a copy of the diplomatic note sent by the Saudi Arabian Ministry of Foreign Affairs that stated "the Ministry of Information as received NO correspondences from the above mentioned". This is in direct contradiction as evidenced by the second paragraph of the April 12, 2000 letter from the First Secretary:

160

"Several years ago, when you first contacted the Embassy, your claim was forwarded to the appropiate authorities in the Kingdom. At this time, the Minister of Information indicated that he knew of no agreement with you. I believe the American Embassy in Riyadh received the same response when it requested information on your behalf. I explained this to you in our telephone conversation."

The First Secretary is accurate on this point. He did convey that message to me. The question is, if several years ago they received correspondence about me from your Embassy, the U.S. State Department and several directly from me, why serveral years later in a diplomatic note, can they claim they still have received "NO correspondence" related to me. My letter of April 26, 1999 sent to the First Secretary was only about this inconsistency and stated dates of the correspondence sent to the Kingdom on many occassions by several sources.

I'm aware that this matter is of far more importance to me and is but one on many, many items that cross the First Secretary's desk, and it would be easy for him not to recall all the information received and thereby understandable he had overlooked the important proof of the legitimacy of my employment to the Kingdom.

There are other points of inconsistency in correspondence from the First Secretary wherein I could prove my employment to the Kingdom, if given an opportunity to present this evidence directly to you for your consideration. One hour of your time would clear up all the inconsistences and allow us to settle this matter quickly. I am more than willing to travel to Washington and meet with you at your convenience.

Haven't I earned a one hour meeting with you on the strength of thirty one months of dedicated service to the Kingdom of Saudi Arabia? Will you please give me this opportunity to explain in detail what I did and first hand check all the evidence of my efforts so we can arrive at a mutual decision.

Sincerely,

James L. Dickson, Jr.
President
J.L. Dickson Associates

JLD/rod
enclosures

James L. Dickson Jr.

SHERWOOD BOEHLERT
23d District, New York

COMMITTEES:
SCIENCE
SUBCOMMITTEE ON BASIC RESEARCH

TRANSPORTATION AND INFRASTRUCTURE
CHAIRMAN, SUBCOMMITTEE ON
WATER RESOURCES AND ENVIRONMENT
SUBCOMMITTEE ON RAILROADS

HOUSE PERMANENT SELECT COMMITTEE
ON INTELLIGENCE

U.S. DELEGATION, NORTH ATLANTIC ASSEMBLY
CHAIRMAN, NORTHEAST AGRICULTURE CAUCUS
CHAIRMAN, MINOR LEAGUE BASEBALL CAUCUS

Congress of the United States
House of Representatives
Washington, DC 20515-3223

WASHINGTON OFFICE:
2246 RAYBURN HOUSE OFFICE BUILDING
WASHINGTON, DC 20515-3223
(202) 225-3665
Fax: (202) 225-1891
E-Mail: rep.boehlert@mail.house.gov

CENTRAL OFFICE:
ALEXANDER PIRNIE FEDERAL BUILDING
10 BROAD STREET
UTICA, NY 13501
(315) 793-8146
Fax: (315) 798-4099

TOLL FREE: 1-800-235-2525

September 7, 2000

Mr. James L. Dickson, Jr.
P.O. Box 271
Hamilton, New York 13346

Dear Mr. Dickson:

I am enclosing a copy of the letter I received from Ms. Larkin in response to my most recent inquiry on your behalf.

As you will note, Ms. Larkin states the Department of State (DoS) has exhausted all options it has at this point in representing your claim with Saudi officials. She indicates that until you have exercised available legal action and/or have additional information to submit for consideration, the department can do nothing further to assist you. Based upon the current situation, Ms. Larkin confirms that the department's position is that there would be no benefit to a personal meeting with DoS staff.

In addition to my written correspondence to DoS, I have spoken with Ms. Larkin and indicated my interest in and support of your efforts to resolve your claim. However, the department continues to maintain its staff has done everything it can to represent your interests.

I sincerely regret this response could not have been more in line with your wishes. I know the amount of time and energy you put into the project itself and efforts to process your claim.

You may keep me updated on any further action you take and as appropriate, I will do what I can to represent your interests.

With warmest regards,

Sincerely,

Sherwood Boehlert
Member of Congress

SB:jd
Enclosure

162

AUG 2 5 2000

United States Department of State

Washington, D.C. 20520

AUG 2 1 2000

Dear Mr. Boehlert,

Thank you for your letter of June 12, concerning the claim against Saudi Arabia of your constituent, James L. Dickson, President of J.L. Dickson Associates. We apologize for the delay in responding.

As you are aware from our several exchanges of correspondence, the Department has worked with Mr. Dickson at length to assist him in pursuing his claim. Since June 1998, the Department has contacted the Saudi Embassy in Washington numerous times, both orally and in writing, on Mr. Dickson's behalf, to provide documents from him and to press for a response. Furthermore, the U.S. Embassy in Riyadh has contacted the Saudi government, transmitted documents from Mr. Dickson, and requested consideration and a response from the Saudi Ministry of Information.

The Saudi Government responded to our Embassy in Riyadh in March 1999, calling Mr. Dickson's claim "completely groundless" as far as records of the Ministry of Information are concerned. An official of the Saudi Embassy in Washington responded in April 2000, stating that he found no documentation "indicating the existence of any agreement between [Mr. Dickson] and any entity of the Saudi government."

We share Mr. Dickson's disappointment with these conclusions. However, as indicated in the Department's letter to you of May 24, the Department is not in a position to pursue this matter any further with the Saudi government, given that Saudi officials have denied the validity of Mr. Dickson's claim, that he has elected not to pursue his claim in Saudi or U.S. courts, and that he has chosen to seek compensation solely by requesting it from Saudi officials.

The Honorable
    Sherwood Boehlert,
        House of Representatives.

163

James L. Dickson Jr.

- 2 -

Under generally accepted principles of international
law and longstanding State Department practice, the U.S.
government can only consider espousing, or formally adopting
as its own, a private claim against another government if
three prerequisites are met: (1) the claim involves a
violation of that state's international responsibilities;
(2) the claimant was a U.S. citizen at the time the claim
arose and continually thereafter to the date of espousal;
(3) the claimant has exhausted available local legal
remedies. Because Mr. Dickson has not met the third of
these requirements, the United States is not in a position
to espouse his claim against the Saudi Government.

Moreover, since any presentation or argument of Mr.
Dickson's claim would be conducted primarily in writing, it
would be best for any additional arguments, evidence or
materials that Mr. Dickson may have to be submitted to the
Department in writing, rather than in a personal meeting.
We have invited him to provide any such additional materials
for our consideration. If appropriate, we will arrange for
Department officials to transmit any new materials to Saudi
authorities on his behalf. If at any time we believe that a
meeting with Mr. Dickson would be helpful to our
consideration of his claim, we will proceed to arrange such
a meeting.

With these considerations in mind, the extensive steps
taken by the Department on Mr. Dickson's behalf are all that
it appropriately can do at this time. In light of the
negative responses from the Saudi Government, there would be
no benefit to Mr. Dickson to arranging for him to meet with
Department officials. We regret that this reply cannot be
more encouraging.

Sincerely,

Barbara Larkin
Assistant Secretary
Legislative Affairs

J. L. DICKSON ASSOCIATES

P.O. Box 271, Hamilton, N.Y. 13346   (315) 824-1535

January 24, 2001

Senator Hillary Rodham Clinton
Senator Dirksen Building
U.S.Senate
Washington DC 20510

Dear Senator:

In July 1999 and again in August 2000 I wrote to you asking for help. I stated that if you were my Senator I would be first in line seeking your assistance. I know I'm not first in line but I'm still convinced that you are one of the few people in government that can quickly resolve my problems with the Kingdom of Saudi Arabia.

I was hired by King Fahd and the Minister of Information Ali Al-Shair from the Kingdom of Saudi Arabia to create a public relations project for them in the United States. I worked 12-16 hour days (many days longer due to the 12 hour time difference) from1990 until late 1992. To this date I have not been paid any monies of the agreed compensation. At issue here is more than the seven figure amount of money owed me. The complexities go far beyond the public relations project and I'm told they are political, not economic or legal, and my only hope of getting paid is to have a high profile american politician be involved. Simply stated, Senator, I need your help.

Any attempt to outline this project or give details of my efforts to resolve the problem would not fairly or accurately give you enough data to help me. It is not possible to send you correspondence, diplomatic notes, etc., that could explain even the last four years of my efforts and these by themselves certainly would not paint an accurate picture.

I'm hoping the seriousness of my problem and all the efforts I've put into it will convince you I'm worthy of helping. A short meeting in Washington DC with you is enough for me to receive a fair hearing, and if at that time you cannot help me I will thank you and move on.

Please find enclosed a copy of my August 19, 2000 letter to you. It will help to explain why I need your help.

Thank you,

James L. Dickson Jr.

165

HILLARY RODHAM CLINTON
NEW YORK
SENATOR

RUSSELL SENATE OFFICE BUILDING
SUITE 476
WASHINGTON, DC 20510-3204
202-224-4451

United States Senate

WASHINGTON, DC 20510–3204

May 30, 2001

Mr. James L. Dickson, Jr.
P.O. Box 271
Hamilton, New York 13346

Dear Mr. Dickson:

Thank you for contacting my office for assistance. The trust and confidence that your request represents is very important to me. A Constituent Liaison has been assigned to handle your matter and you should be hearing from a member of my staff very soon.

Sincerely yours,

Hillary Rodham Clinton

Hillary Rodham Clinton

HRC/jlk/gbs

166

HILLARY RODHAM CLINTON
NEW YORK
SENATOR

RUSSELL SENATE OFFICE BUILDING
SUITE 476
WASHINGTON, DC 20510–3204
202–224–4451

United States Senate

WASHINGTON, DC 20510–3204

October 2, 2001

Mr. James L. Dickson, Jr.
P.O. Box 271
Hamilton, New York 13346

Dear Mr. Dickson:

    I am writing in response to your request of assistance regarding your dispute with the government of Saudi Arabia. On your behalf, Senator Clinton's office contacted the Department of State for guidance in this matter. Enclosed is a copy of their response.

    In his correspondence to Senator Clinton's office, Assistant Secretary Paul Kelly explains that the Department of State has contacted the Saudi Government on numerous occasions regarding your claim. In response to the Department's requests, the Saudi Government denied your claims and indicated that you were unable to provide evidence of a contract.

    According to Mr. Kelly, the Department advised that you contact an attorney, if you wish to pursue this matter further, and provided you with a list of attorneys in Saudi Arabia. At this time, the Department of State is unable to pursue this matter further with Saudi officials, due to the fact that you have not sought a legal remedy to this dispute. For your convenience, I have enclosed an additional copy of the list of attorneys provided by the Department of State.

    Please be assured that Senator Clinton's office has done all it possibly can to assist you and that your case has received a thorough review.

Sincerely yours,

Jennifer Kritz

Jennifer Kritz
Constituent Liaison

167

James L. Dickson Jr.

United States Department of State

Washington, D.C. 20520

JUN 25 2001

Dear Senator Clinton,

Thank you for your letter of May 30 concerning your constituent, Mr. James L. Dickson, Jr., President of J. L. Dickson Associates. The Department of State is aware of Mr. Dickson's dispute with the Government of Saudi Arabia and has raised his concerns with the Saudi Government on several occasions.

Since June 1998, the Department has contacted the Saudi Embassy in Washington numerous times, both orally and in writing, concerning Mr. Dickson's claim. We have provided documents from him to the Saudi Embassy and sought a response. The U.S. Embassy in Riyadh has also contacted the Saudi government, transmitted documents from Mr. Dickson, and pressed for a response from the Saudi Ministry of Information. The U.S. Embassy provided Mr. Dickson with a list of lawyers in Saudi Arabia who might be able to assist him if he decided to pursue local remedies.

In response to the Department's requests, the Saudi Government responded to our Embassy in Riyadh in March 1999, characterizing Mr. Dickson's claim as "completely groundless," based on records of its Ministry of Information. In April 2000, an official of the Saudi Embassy in Washington stated that, based on materials supplied by Mr. Dickson, he found no "documentation indicating the existence of any agreement between [Mr. Dickson] and any entity of the Saudi government," and that the Ministry of Information "knew of no agreement with [Mr. Dickson]."

We understand Mr. Dickson is disappointed with these conclusions. However, given that Saudi officials have denied the validity of Mr. Dickson's claim, that he has elected not to pursue this matter in Saudi or U.S. courts, and has chosen to seek compensation solely by requesting it from Saudi officials, the Department is not in a position to pursue this matter any further with the Saudi Government.

The Honorable
    Hillary Rodham Clinton,
      United States Senate.

-2-

This decision reflects generally accepted principles of international law and longstanding State Department practice, pursuant to which the U.S. Government can only consider espousing, or formally adopting as its own, a private claim against another government if three prerequisites are met: (1) the claim involves a violation of that state's international responsibilities; (2) the claimant was a U.S. citizen at the time that the claim arose and continually thereafter to the date of espousal; and (3) the claimant has exhausted available local legal remedies.

Should Mr. Dickson decide to pursue a claim in Saudi Arabia, the Department stands ready to provide ordinary consular assistance, and encourages him to keep the Department apprised of its progress and result. In Washington, the Department's Office of Overseas Citizens Services, which may be reached at (202) 736-4953, can provide him with a list of attorneys in Saudi Arabia who may be able to provide him with legal assistance.

We hope this information will be useful to you in responding to your constituent. Please let us know if we can be of further assistance.

Sincerely,

Paul V. Kelly
Assistant Secretary
Legislative Affairs

Enclosure:
    Correspondence returned.

About the Author:

James Dickson has been a consultant for a wide variety of clients both in and out of the U.S. for over twenty-five years. He has helped his clients buy, improve and create new businesses. Dickson served as Chairman of the Board of a New York Corporation, President of a Massachusetts Corporation, as well as President of J.L. Dickson Associates. His client list includes commercial corporations, government agencies and two governors. His trip to Saudi Arabia was to meet his Saudi partner, expand his partners business and set up new businesses in the Gulf Region. He was doing this when he was asked by King Fahd and Minister Al-Shair of the Kingdom of Saudi Arabia to create a Public Relations Project for the Saudis in the United States.

Printed in the United States
1322500005B/65